THE

AMAZING ADVENTURES

OF

PERCH THE CAT

ANTHONY KESSEL

ILLUSTRATED BY LEONE KESSEL

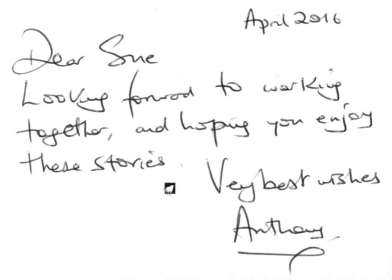

April 2016

Dear Sue
Looking forward to working
together, and hoping you enjoy
these stories.

Very best wishes

Anthony

Matador
9 Priory Business Park,
Wistow Road, Kibworth Beauchamp,
Leicestershire. LE8 0RX
Tel: (+44) 116 279 2299
Fax: (+44) 116 279 2277
Email: books@troubador.co.uk
Web: www.troubador.co.uk/matador

ISBN 978 1848767 591

British Library Cataloguing in Publication Data.
A catalogue record for this book is available from the British Library.

Typeset in 10pt Aldine401 BT Roman by Troubador Publishing Ltd, Leicester, UK

Matador is an imprint of Troubador Publishing Ltd

Printed and bound in the UK by TJ International, Padstow, Cornwall

*For my truly remarkable daughter Leone – the
inspiration behind these stories and, without
whom, there would be no Perch.*

Acknowledgements

One Friday night, several years ago, I was sitting on my daughter Leone's bed preparing to tell her a story. An end-of-the-week tale had already been a ritual for a while by then, but that night was different as I conjured the first adventure about a ginger cat called Perch. Further Perch stories were told on many Friday nights over a number of years, absorbed by an audience of one – but what a startling audience, with a vivid imagination and a thirst for creativity. Leone is truly the inspiration behind these stories, the attentive ears but also the enraptured soul who has fuelled my own passion.

My daughter is not, however, the only source of energy behind this book. One evening after dinner, a year or so after the inception of Perch, my wife, Elizabeth, asked me to recount the story that I had told Leone earlier that evening. Elizabeth was so taken by the adventure that appears in this book as 'The Curse of Crazybones' that she encouraged me to start writing the stories down. Which I did, and slowly those stories have morphed into this book. So my second acknowledgement is to my gorgeous wife for her ongoing encouragement and support for this project – as well as for the many hours she has spent editing and advising on various chapter versions. She is also the co-author of chapter six 'Behind Bars (Again)'.

While all the Perch stories have been conceived in my

imagination, one particular adventure has drawn on a shared experience. My dear friend Peter Oppenheimer will undoubtedly find familiarity in 'The Catlas Mountains', though the cats of course were not present when we attempted to climb Mount Toubkal over two decades ago.

Finally, in a bigger sense, this endeavour would have been impossible without my mother. She has always been such a supporter of me, through her steadfast presence, immense love and unswerving belief in my abilities. Her recent tragic death has left a terrible hole in my life, but the strength that her faith has instilled very much remains.

Contents

Chapter 1

A Cat Called Perch

One bright morning in early spring, a ginger cat rubbed her eyes as she slowly woke up. After a few moments she sighed, as she once again saw the same bars that had been there for as long as she could remember. In fact, this ginger cat couldn't remember anything except for life inside her cage in a pet shop in north London.

But the soft ginger cat had always had very active thoughts. More like dreams really. Well, to be even more precise, one dream. It's the same dream that she'd had every night for as long as she could remember – the dream that one day, yes one day, she would be one of the cats from the shop chosen to go to a new home with a new owner.

The ginger cat was no fool though. She knew that it couldn't be any old owner. She needed a kind and caring owner. Over the past few weeks she'd watched what had happened to other cats in the shop. They all wanted to get out, but sometimes getting out could be worse than staying in.

She remembered her best friend, Fortune, for instance, a tabby cat who used to be in the next cage. Fortune wanted to get out so much that she used to purr, a little desperately, at every person who came into the shop looking for a mog. She also used to try and chew through the bars of the cage. Eventually, a man came into the shop with a boy called Owen, who was about seven years old.

'Which one d'ya fancy?' said the boy's father. He seemed in a hurry.

Owen, who looked like a bit of a meany, glanced around at all the cages. After a while, he fixed his stare on Fortune.

'I'll … have … this one,' he said coldly. His nose was so close that it was almost touching the cage.

The way Owen spoke made the ginger cat shiver. Fortune looked happy enough when she left the shop with Owen but, a week later, Owen's father brought her back. The ginger cat remembered Fortune's sad expression when she returned. For twelve days Fortune didn't say a word and, to be honest, she was never the same again. The ginger cat had learned a valuable lesson. You must pick your owner very carefully and, most importantly, you need somebody kind.

On that sunny morning, the first day in April, a man called Charles Needle, known affectionately as Charlie, was walking merrily down his street. Charlie was thirty-one years old, and was a tall man with cropped blonde hair. He used to have hair that went all the way down to his shoulders, but he cut it short after the long locks got in his eyes and made him drop an important cricket catch. That was a couple of years ago, when Charlie was captain of the England cricket team and couldn't afford any more such mistakes. Although no longer captain, Charlie was still a professional cricketer and had kept his hair short. He owned a small house in a road called Cecile Park – he always thought it was a bit strange having a road called Park, but there were lots of odd names like that in London.

Charlie was particularly happy as he strode down the street

because it was the day that he was going to buy himself a pet cat. He had thought about getting himself a cat for some time, but now he was finally going to do it. And the reason was simple – he needed company. Charlie's main home was in the north of England, where his wife and children lived. He only used their Crouch End house for cricket matches and other important meetings in London.

Charlie missed his family dearly whenever he was away. There was one thing, however, that always provided comfort in their absence, and that was the photographs that Charlie had carefully placed on the mantelpiece. There was one with his wife, Anna, on their wedding day; she looked so beautiful in her bridal gown. There was a photograph of his daughters, Minnie and Leila, on the beach in Newquay, spades in one hand and ice creams in the other; and another of little Eli, his son, holding aloft a cricket ball, beaming with pride.

After much pondering, Charlie had decided that a furry companion would help him feel less lonely. Besides, he had wanted a cat ever since he was a little boy – and now he was going to get one.

Charlie reached the end of Cecile Park and turned right, down towards the centre of Crouch End. As he got closer, the only thing Charlie had to decide was where to buy his cat. The nearest place was Peter's Pet Shop on the high street, but recently Peter's twin brother had opened a similar store around the corner, and had called it Percy's Pet Shop. Brothers can be so competitive, thought Charlie. He decided on Peter's, which was nearer, and gently opened the door.

The bell rang in the pet shop each time a new customer walked in and, whenever it did, all the cats jumped up excitedly. On this morning, the ginger cat had only just finished rubbing her sleepy eyes when she heard the sound. Without thinking, she pounced to the front of her cage and bent her neck, trying to see who had come into the shop.

The ginger cat could just about make out a very tall man, with blonde hair under a black cap, although she couldn't see him very clearly. But what he looked like didn't matter when she heard his voice. He had the most calm, kindly voice she had ever heard. Even more importantly, she knew that voice because she had heard it in her dreams. That was the voice of the man who came to save her. She was sure and listened intently.

'I'd like to buy a cat,' said Charlie.

'Well, you've come to the right place for that,' replied Peter the pet shop owner, with a slight grin.

The ginger cat watched intently as the tall man looked at the row of cages lined up against the wall. Charlie had decided that the best thing to do would be to walk slowly past each cage and to follow his instincts. He would know when he had seen the right cat for him.

The cat in the first cage, a gorgeous white Persian, was exotic and alluring. Charlie imagined spending hours stroking her fur while watching the TV. But she was long-haired and Charlie couldn't help but worry about his sofa.

In the second cage the cat was fast asleep, which wasn't a good sign. But as Charlie reached the next cage, he was forced to stop at the sight of a beautiful grey Siamese, who stared at Charlie with pale blue eyes. She came right up to the front of the cage and then turned to walk sideways by the bars, as if showing off her stunning body. Backwards and forwards she

4

gracefully went. She could be on the catwalk, thought Charlie. He was clearly captivated, and the ginger cat was getting anxious.

Charlie turned to Peter. 'How much is the Siamese?' he asked.

'She isn't cheap,' came the reply.

'I can see that,' said Charlie.

'She's twenty-five pounds.'

In spite of the cost, Charlie was pretty sure he had made his choice, but he felt he should at least see the last few cages. The next two had pretty cats in, but they were no contest for the Siamese. One cage to go.

As Charlie came up to the last cage it seemed a bit different. It was darker inside than the others. So he bent over and leaned forwards to peer inside. At first Charlie couldn't really see anything, but slowly his eyes adjusted and then he could pick out two blue-green pearls suspended in the air. And around those amazing eyes was the loveliest face and body he had ever seen.

She was a ginger cat, and her beauty was in her simplicity. Every object has its perfect form, thought Charlie as he remembered his Greek lessons at school, and she was surely the perfect cat. And she wasn't trying at all, she was just sitting and waiting, but her eyes seemed to speak to Charlie. The ginger cat's stare seemed to be saying, "If you look after me well, I will love you with all my heart."

'How much is this one?' asked Charlie.

Peter seemed surprised. 'Oh, she's not for sale,' he said apologetically.

'Why not?' said Charlie, somewhat concerned.

'She's different, she's … special. And I promised someone I'd look after her myself.'

'How is she special?'

'I can't really explain,' Peter remarked. 'But you would know if you spent time with her – she's just not like other cats.'

Charlie wanted her even more. 'Come on,' he prompted. 'Every cat has its price.'

Peter thought about how much he wanted a new sign for the front of his shop – Percy's sign was so much bigger. Perhaps if he sold the cat he could afford it.

'One hundred pounds,' he blurted out. That was much more money than Charlie had wanted to spend. But his heart would allow only one thing. He reached into his wallet and counted, as the ginger cat looked on, expectantly. Ten, twenty, thirty … ninety in total.

'I've only got ninety pounds,' he put to Peter questioningly.

Peter shook his head, and the disappointed ginger cat slumped back sadly. It wasn't enough. Charlie felt very low, but there was nothing he could do, and if he went to get more money, the cat might be sold by the time he came back. He muttered to Peter that he would have to go around the corner to Percy's and buy something there, but Peter wouldn't change his price.

So Charlie walked sadly to the door and, just before he got there, sunk his hands in his pockets in preparation for the fresh air outside. As he was opening the door he realised his right hand was touching some paper deep in his pocket. He gripped his fingers and pulled. His hand came out and Charlie realised that he was holding a ten-pound note. There was a soft purr from the far cage. Now he had the full amount.

Just then, Charlie remembered the night before in the Italian restaurant on the high street. The bill had arrived for his pasta but he hadn't been able to find his wallet. Somewhat stumped, Charlie hadn't known what to do when a dark stranger had walked over, as if to help. The stranger had handed him a carefully folded up ten-pound note. Charlie was embarrassed and had tried to look at the man's face, but it was hidden in the shadow of his wide-brimmed hat. The stranger had looked Charlie straight in the eyes and had said, a little magically, 'Keep this, my friend, you'll be needing it.'

Charlie had put the money in his pocket and had been distracted as he noticed his wallet, which had fallen onto the floor. He had looked up to say thank you, but the man was gone.

So Charlie was able to give Peter the one hundred pounds and, in return, Charlie was handed the feline bundle that would change his life.

The next few days passed in a haze for the ginger cat. She was shown her new home, a three-bedroom house on a quiet street that was lined with pretty pink blossom trees, just about to burst into bud. It was more than she had ever dreamt of. There was plenty of space to climb and jump and play, and she couldn't have been happier.

There were three parts of the house of which the ginger cat was particularly fond. She adored her basket, where she would curl up at the end of each day and drift off peacefully to sleep, watched over reassuringly by the family photos on the mantelpiece. The basket was next to the fire in the lounge and was lined with a soft woollen blanket. She also liked Charlie's bedroom, with its big bed, where she would snuggle up in the morning while she waited for Charlie to wake up.

But it was the garden that really captured her heart. Every time she wandered through the kitchen door cat-flap and into the garden, the open space reminded her of her freedom. There was a small lawn, and at the back was a rock garden around a beautiful pond. Charlie had kindly got her some friends, four large fish that lived in the pond. She could tell them apart and knew their names: Orange-tail, Yellow-back, Lightning (who could swim very fast), and Razorback. Some people say that cats prefer to eat fish than to befriend them, but don't you believe it – she loved those fish.

The ginger cat soon got into a routine with her new life and her fish friends. Each day would pass easily: breakfast and hanging out in the morning, perhaps some chores in the afternoon, then off with Charlie for an evening walk around the block; he always liked to keep active. And when she came home she would go straight into the garden with a night-time fish food snack for her pond pals.

Life was looking good, but there was one thing that troubled our ginger cat, and that was that she didn't have a name. She knew Charlie was thinking about it because she saw scribbled lists on paper around the house. But one's name is very important, because it says something about who you really are, and sometimes she would wake up at night in a sweat, desperately hoping that the nameless days would soon come to an end. Perhaps Charlie was waiting for something special, for some inspiration, she thought.

It was in the middle of such a night that the ginger cat woke up with a start. At first she heard nothing but then, with her ears pricked up, she could just make out a quiet, high-pitched cry. It was like a sort of screeching and, as she turned her head gently from side to side, she realised that it was coming from the garden. It was a cry for help. The fish were in trouble.

There was a blur of ginger fur as she bounded through the cat-flap into the garden and raced towards the pond. As she got closer she heard splashing and could make out an animal at the side of the pond. He was putting his paw in and out of the water trying to scoop the fish into his mouth. He turned to look at the approaching cat and bared his sharp teeth. He clearly did not like having his dinner disturbed. The ginger cat had heard about these urban foxes – they could be mean, and they would eat anything.

The fox growled loudly, and the ginger cat was scared. She took a deep breath in, and let out the loudest, meanest meeeeowwww she had ever made. She even frightened herself. The fox looked surprised. He turned on his heels and sloped off, but not without glancing deliberately over his shoulder as if to say, "I'll be back."

The ginger cat sighed with relief and looked at the pond. She counted four fish – thankfully they were all still alive. She sat down to catch her breath, and then, something really quite extraordinary happened. As she was watching her fish friends, she noticed bubbles coming from their mouths and up through the water, many more of them than normal. First she thought it was because of the trouble with the fox, but then she noticed a pattern. The bubbles were coming together at the surface and spelt the words *Hungry fox, please help*.

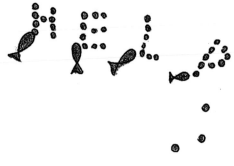

The cat knew straight away that she had to do something. It was morning now, and they would be alright in the daytime, as the fox would only come again in the dark. But the following night, as soon as she was back from her evening walk and Charlie was asleep, she went back into the garden and got straight to work.

In the big oak tree next to the pond the ginger cat built a ledge. It was in the branches about halfway up the tree and would be her look-out point, so she could see the fox coming. And all around the pond she trailed string from the shed and attached bells to it. If the fox came to the pond looking for food he would touch the string, which would ring the bells and the ginger watch-cat would be alerted. She placed a strong stick, her weapon, on the ledge beside her in the tree, and waited … and waited.

In the very middle of the night, our ginger cat awoke with a start. She had been dreaming of sitting on a bench listening to church bells ringing. She was confused as she came out of the dream and saw where she was, and she could still hear the church bells. Then, she realised what was happening – the fox had triggered her alarm.

She shone her torch towards the ground and could see the fox leaning over the pond. He was grabbing at the water and had Orange-tail in his paws. Orange-tail was wriggling and was slippery but was almost in the fox's mouth. His teeth were glistening in the torchlight and were wet in anticipation. Orange-tail looked up at the ginger cat, who knew she had one chance and had to act right now.

She meowed as loud as she could, and the fox looked up over his shoulder. He snarled and growled back at her, then returned to his dinner. He was about to bite down on Orange-tail when the ginger cat picked up her stick and threw it with all her strength. The stick hit the fox right on his bottom, making him lose his balance and fall on his face into the mud by the pond. Shocked and filthy, the fox scampered off as quickly as he could, never to return.

But the fox wasn't the only one to lose his balance. The cat

11

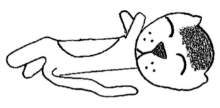 made such an effort when she threw the stick that the ledge wobbled, then wobbled some more, and she lost her footing and fell through the air to the ground below. She landed next to the tree and was knocked out.

When Charlie woke up the next morning, at first he was just a little surprised that the ginger cat wasn't on his bed. But after a while he started to get worried. He looked in all the bedrooms but she wasn't there. He imagined she might be in the kitchen finishing off the milk from the fridge, but she wasn't. Her basket was empty, and the blanket wasn't even warm.

By lunchtime Charlie was getting really worried and, as he tried to eat something, he stared blankly out of the kitchen window. Then he remembered – he hadn't checked the garden. Charlie jumped up and went outside. She wasn't on the lawn, so he wandered towards the pond, where there was a lot of string and water around. He thought the gardener must have been up to something.

Then, out of the corner of his eye Charlie noticed a ginger blob on the ground by the tree. He ran over and picked her up. She was cold, but alive. Charlie rubbed her fur and slowly his friend woke up. They stared into each other's eyes lovingly.

'I was so worried,' said Charlie with a tear in the corner of his eye.

The ginger cat blinked warmly into her owner's eyes and

nuzzled her small face into his neck. She felt so cared for cradled in Charlie's arms and purred loudly. Just then, they both caught sight of something peculiar. There were six bright eyes watching them from the neighbour's garden. They belonged to three cats sitting stock still, observing the scene with what appeared to be real concern.

'Hello, you lot,' chirped Charlie. The ginger cat stared at Charlie quizzically, as if to say, "Who are they?"

'Well, if I'm not mistaken, this is Greystoke,' said Charlie, pointing out a solid-looking British Blue. 'And that's Bells, who lives down the road,' he continued while indicating a lovely looking Siamese. 'And I think that striking Burmese is Snapper from the house around the corner.'

The bundle in his arms looked very pleased. 'You won't be short of friends then,' said Charlie quietly, as he stroked her with great affection.

The ginger cat climbed up Charlie's strong arms, as if she wanted to say something to him. Her mouth was close to his ear when she noticed movement in the pond behind him. Bubbles were floating up from the bottom, and as they reached the surface the bubbles formed letters that spelt one word: *T–h–a–n–k–s*.

As the ginger cat smiled, Charlie suddenly remembered his manners. He had completely forgotten to introduce her back to the cats in the neighbour's garden.

'I'm so sorry,' he whispered in the ginger cat's ear. 'Everybody, I want you to meet … to meet …. to meet …' But he still didn't have a name. Charlie looked up and saw the ledge, then looked down and saw the fish in the pond. Ledge, fish, ledge, fish … something was coming to him.

'Everybody,' he said again, 'I want you to meet … Perch the cat.'

Perch's whiskers spread out as she smiled from ear to ear. She was very happy. And there's one thing you can be sure of – that night, she slept very well indeed.

Chapter 2

The Legend of the Magic Cat

One warm late spring day, Perch woke up to the sound of birds chirping in the big old oak tree in the garden. She stretched out her four paws and went into the kitchen for a nice bowl of full cream milk. Charlie was always encouraging her to eat healthily, but an occasional luxury was allowed. As Perch enjoyed her delicious drink, she realised that she was feeling a little out of sorts and wondered if she had got out of her basket on the wrong side.

Perch popped herself up onto the sofa and sat to have a think. The last few weeks had been incredible. She was thrilled to be in her new home and adored Charlie. Although she liked it best when he was around, whenever Charlie was up north with his family he always left plenty of food and made sure a friend checked in on her. Perch liked the neighbourhood in Crouch End and loved her new cat friends.

Bells, for instance, was a sweet and playful cat, not at all like some of the other Siamese cats that Perch had met in her days in the pet shop. They had been fickle and moody, but Bells was always in good spirits. She could be a bit scatty at times, getting into muddles, and was surprisingly clumsy for her breed, but one look at her sweet, pretty face and you could forgive her anything.

Greystoke, on the other hand, was careful, organised, and was rather clever too. She was a dependable friend, who was always good in a crisis. Greystoke's owner, Professor Setting from down the road, was a retired anthropologist, who used to teach at the university about the history of different civilizations, like the Romans and the Egyptians. He doted on his beloved cat with her soft blue-grey fur, and he read to Greystoke well into the night about adventures in faraway lands. He also liked slipping her sweet treats under the table at mealtimes, which was why she was quite portly around the middle and always preferred to do things nice and slow – which suited Perch just fine.

Snapper, however, never did anything slowly. Where other cats walked he raced, climbed and jumped – always on the move and always ready for action. He was the bravest and toughest cat Perch had ever met, and hanging around with him always meant something unexpected and fun was just around the corner. Perch had a soft spot for Snapper's rugged charm and dark looks, although sometimes he was a bit rash and his excitabile nature got him into trouble.

While Perch was thinking how happy she was with her new friends, Greystoke appeared at the kitchen window. Every day since the meeting by the pond in Charlie's garden they had been out together, going for walks and just getting to know each other better. Today they were taking a trip to Hornsey library.

'Are you ready?' asked Greystoke.

'In a moment,' replied Perch.

'OK,' said Greystoke. 'But don't be too long. If we get going now, and allow exactly twelve minutes to get there, then we'll still have an hour and a quarter before the library closes.'

'But we've got to pick up Bells and Snapper on the way,'

reminded Perch.

'I've accounted for that in
my calculations,' came the
smart response.

A few minutes later, the
four cats were strolling down
Gladwell Road towards the library and were chat chat chatting
away. Bells was telling a funny story about her two younger
sisters, Poppy and Angel, who lived with her at number ninety-
four.

'And then Poppy,' she giggled, 'knocked the bag of flour off
the shelf and it fell all over her body … she looked like a

Snowcat!'
The others roared with
laughter. 'And then Angel,'
continued Bells, who was just
about controlling her giggles,

'squirted the glue and it stuck all the flour to Poppy's fur. They
spent three hours in the shower getting it off!'

Perch thought Bells was very lucky. The Mason family,
where Bells lived, were major cat lovers and couldn't bear to
separate the sisters. Bells also got to visit her mum and brother
Henry twice a year on the Mason family trips to see Auntie
Chloe in Cornwall. They were a very close family.

Snapper quickly joined in, sharing a story about his Great
Uncle Augustine, an adventurer who really had come face to
face with a Snowcat on one of his Arctic expeditions. A real hero
in the Snapper family, Great Uncle Augustine had walked and
swum all the way from Greece during the Second World War to
start a new life in England. Perch could see where Snapper got
his fighting spirit from.

Then Greystoke piped in with a story of her beloved father, Horace, who had been the official mouse-catcher at Lauderdale House in Highgate for seventeen years.

'He must have caught a lot of mice in that time,' added Perch.

'Hardly any,' replied Greystoke. 'He wasn't scary in the slightest, but they adored him all the same. He spent most of his time in the huge library, reading book after book. He was very brainy and founded an organisation called MOGSA.'

'MOGSA?' asked Bells. 'What's that?'

'It's for cats with an IQ in the upper five per cent of the normal distribution for feline intelligence,' explained Greystoke. 'I'm a member.'

'I've no idea what that means,' said Bells. 'But, can I join?'

Greystoke had to think quickly on her paws, and didn't want to upset Bells. 'I'll have to look into it and get back to you,' she responded.

'But what happened to your dad?' interrupted Snapper.

'Oh,' said Greystoke abruptly. 'When he finally retired he went to live with the professor before moving to the Canary Islands with a much younger lady friend. I haven't seen him since.'

'Now it's your turn,' beckoned Bells cheerfully to Perch.

But there was a stony silence and Bells realised her mistake. Snapper stopped in his tracks and Greystoke looked awkwardly down at her paws. Bells had forgotten that Perch knew nothing about her own family and had no stories to share.

'Hey look, we're here,' said Snapper brightly as they reached the library, trying to change the subject.

But Perch had become very quiet and sad. She told the others she would meet up with them later as she wanted to find something special in the library, but really it was because she needed to spend a little time by herself.

Perch sneaked into the library behind two noisy people, careful not to be seen by the librarian, who would shoo her out, and wandered over to the cookery section. In the first book she looked at there were recipes for some of her favourite meals: grilled sardines on toast with a glass of semi-skimmed milk; roasted Highgate wood-pigeon on a bed of cat biscuits; and ice-cream sundae (though she liked to eat it every day of the week). But even these tasty treats didn't cheer her up.

In search of something to take her away, Perch went over to the history section. She loved losing herself in a book about the olden days and sensed that was what she needed. Deciding to leave her choice to chance, Perch closed her eyes and felt the books along the history shelf. Eventually her paw fell on one that felt different to the others. Perch pulled it out and sat down at the desk.

The book she had chosen had a beautiful multi-coloured front cover and Perch immediately noticed the title, *The Legend of the Magic Cat*. She opened it up. The first page had something that Perch had never seen before, and that seemed rather strange. It said, "Enter at Reader's Risk". A little bit nervous, but also excited, she turned the next page, and in the middle it said, "If You Like Adventures Press Here", and it had a sort of circle underneath. Perch paused for a moment and thought, Well, I do like adventures, and placed her paw gently on the circle.

The first thing Perch realised was that her paw had gone

right through the circle, and now her arm was being sucked into the book. There was a loud whoosh and a flash as Perch felt

 herself going further in and then everything went dark and silent. She had wanted to lose herself in a good book, but

this was a bit more than Perch had expected.

After what seemed like an awfully long time, and feeling a little dizzy, Perch tentatively opened her eyes. She looked around and couldn't quite believe what she was seeing. She certainly wasn't in Hornsey library, but instead was sitting in the middle of a field, in the middle of the countryside and it was a bit damp under her bottom. Oh, I hate the wet and mud, she thought, and was about to lick her fur clean when she decided that it probably wasn't a very good idea.

Perch glanced around and noticed what looked like a village in the distance, with smoke coming out of some of the small houses. With her tummy rumbling she set off towards the houses, dodging the sheep and cows, and with her paws sinking deep into the mud with each step. When she made it to the end of the field she sighed with relief. That is, until she saw what was in front of her.

The village was very strange. The tiny houses didn't look anything like Charlie's solid red brick home in Crouch End. They were more like huts, and the roofs seemed to be made of straw. There were animals everywhere – lots of dogs, some looking quite nasty, as well as pigs and horses. And they were peeing and pooing wherever they liked. It stank! There were no roads, no cars, and no lights. Everything was different, and Perch was very, very confused.

Perch climbed up onto a straw roof to have a think. She felt lonely up there. As she was trying to work out what had happened, she remembered a TV programme about medieval times. The houses looked a bit like this, but the medieval times were a long, long time ago.

As Perch sat and pondered a little boy came over and, standing at the bottom of the house, he started purring at her.

''Ere luverly pussy,' he beckoned with his finger. 'Come down to Tommy.'

He was a sweet-looking boy, about six years old but dressed in dirty clothes with hands and face to match. Most striking though were his teeth, which were terrible. By golly, thought Perch, he really needs to see the dentist.

Tommy seemed kind and unassuming, which meant a lot to Perch, so she said hello and asked him politely if he could tell her where she was. What happened next was most peculiar though, as Tommy jumped in surprise, and fell backwards onto the muddy path.

'You … can … sp … sp … speak …' he stammered.

'Well, obviously I can,' said Perch, surprised by her own communication skills.

'But … how comes … I … don't understand,' continued Tommy.

After a while, Tommy settled down and got used to the thought of speaking to Perch. He told her about his village, and the other villages over the hills; and about the Baron, in his big,

big house, who owned all the land. Everybody in the village had to give their money to the Baron to live on his land. And there was never enough food, except for at the Baron's house. The Baron got fatter and fatter with his castle feasts, while Tommy's tummy always felt empty.

'And what about your friends?' asked Perch.

And that's when Tommy stopped and looked solemnly down at his toes.

'I used to have a lot of friends,' he said, 'but one by one they've been … taken away.'

'What do you mean, taken away? Do you mean to school?' said Perch.

She could see that Tommy looked frightened and hardly wanted to answer this. But she needed to know, so she gently asked him again.

'Tommy, were they taken to see their grandparents, or people in another village?'

'No,' said Tommy, 'it's the D … D … .' He could hardly say the word. 'It's the Drag …. Drag … Dragon. The Rhyming Dragon. If people don't pay their money to the Baron, he sets the Rhyming Dragon on us – sends the beast out at night to

swipe 'annover kiddie. Loads of 'em that goggle-eyed monster's got, all me friends. And we never see the little ones again.'

'The Rhyming Dragon,' Perch replied. 'Dragons don't exist, they're just stories from olden times …' And as she said the words the thought formed in Perch's mind – perhaps she was *in* the olden times.

But then Tommy seemed to perk up a little. His eyes widened, and he stared intently at Perch, as if he knew something important.

'I've heard about you,' he said. 'Thank the 'eavens and the stars. You're the Legend of the Magic Cat, the cat who talks and slays the evil Dragon. My parents, and their parents, and even their parents have all talked about the legend – the cat that will save us all.'

Perch giggled and was about to tell Tommy that she was just an ordinary cat, who had never done anything very brave in her life, but, before she got a chance, Tommy was running down the muddy street shouting, 'The Magic Cat, the Magic Cat, it's here.'

Somewhat confused, Perch leapt off the roof to go after Tommy. But before she could catch up with him to explain the misunderstanding, there was an almighty thud, as a ball of matted fur splashed in a puddle right in front of her.

'Bells?' said Perch, astonished. 'What on earth are you doing here?'

'That's what I was going to ask you,' said Bells.

'Well, I asked first,' replied Perch.

Before the conversation could go any further Perch looked over Bells' shoulder and saw Snapper and Greystoke barrelling down the street towards her in a slide of mud. They landed with a splat in the same puddle.

'Wow,' said Snapper. 'I can't wait to do that again.' And then he saw Perch. They all had the biggest, best hug that Perch could ever remember.

The cats explained how they had grown concerned for Perch and had followed her over to the history section in the library. Bells had noticed the multi-coloured book and had picked it up and been sucked in. Snapper hurtled afterwards and Greystoke, though it all looked a bit dangerous, didn't want to miss out.

'But how did you know I was in the village?' asked Perch.

'Well, you know how clever Greystoke is,' Snapper came in. 'She followed your paw-prints in the mud, which led us in this direction.'

Perch glanced at Greystoke, who was looking rather pleased with herself. Then, just as she was about to tell them how odd and old everything was here, a bell rang out. All the people in the village came running out of their houses and were walking towards the central square. The cats followed, and on the way over Perch told the others all the nonsense about the Rhyming Dragon and the Legend of the Magic Cat. They all thought it was very funny.

Just before they reached the square, Perch looked around because Greystoke had disappeared. Perch shouted and Greystoke answered, 'I'm over here,' and she really was close by, on top of a large rock. But the rock was grey, the same colour as she was, so it was hard to see her.

Greystoke was trying to pull something out of the rock. She tugged and tugged, but gave up. 'I'll help you,' said Perch, who jumped up, put one paw on what looked like a handle, and easily pulled a dark grey metal sword out of the rock. 'This might come in handy with the dragon,' joked Perch, and they all laughed and laughed.

Finally, they reached the area where all the people had gathered. An old man was standing on a sort of stage. He was talking to all the people of the village, who were listening carefully.

'My folks,' he announced. 'We were told by the sorcerer that this day would come. It is the legend of our ancestors, the myth of the day when the magic cat, the cat who talks, rescues our village from the clutches of the cruel dragon who steals our children.'

Perch could hear the words magic cat being whispered over and over, so the cats stayed at the back of the crowd hoping they wouldn't be noticed.

'Hold on,' said Greystoke. 'Remember the book in the library. The book was called *The Legend of the Magic Cat*. It's your story, Perch, the story you fell into, and we're all here to tell it. Don't you see?'

'Oh my,' said Perch quietly. 'I wonder what happens in the end …'

Interrupting her thoughts, the old man beckoned the cats forwards, and people cleared the way for them to walk to the stage. Some people reached over to try to touch them. The old man guided them up the steps and told them his name was Arnold. He noticed the sword in Perch's paw, and looked pleased.

'Look, the magic cat has taken the sword from the stone, just as the legend says.' People started clapping and cheering.

'The Rhyming Dragon lives over there,' Arnold told Perch. 'In Dunkel Beech Woods. Be careful, and good luck.'

'But I'm not the cat you think I am,' said Perch. 'I'm just a regular street cat from Crouch End. The bravest thing I ever did was scare away a fox from our garden.'

But nobody cared and a strong-looking man, the village blacksmith, came through the crowd up onto the stage, holding three more short metal swords. He told the cats he had made the swords himself. They were still hot, straight out of the fire, and each had its own scabbard. He wrapped a strap around each of the cats, so the swords were lying comfortably on their backs.

Snapper looked very excited. Perch was about to say something again, but Arnold interrupted.

'It's your destiny, my friends, now off you go. And God speed!'

As the four brave cats entered Dunkel Beech Woods, Snapper took command. He told them that he would be at the front, then Bells and Greystoke, with Perch at the back.

'Diamond formation,' he said. 'Be absolutely quiet, and look out for my signals.' Snapper had watched a lot of action films.

After about twenty minutes, Snapper raised his paw for them all to stop. He motioned with a straight right paw for Bells to go to the right and held his left paw out for Greystoke to go out left. Perch joined Snapper in the middle and they were all in a line. They walked forwards together very slowly, because Snapper had seen some chimney smoke in the trees ahead …

Just a few yards further and they were able to make out a very big wooden barn, with a garden and fence around it. There was a sign at the entrance that had the picture of a dragon, and underneath it read:

> *It may not be Rome,*
> *But it's Home, Sweet Home.*

With its body half in the barn and half in the garden, the huge dragon lay sleeping. Perch could just make out that there were several large dragon eggs, each about the size of a beach ball, in the straw next to the dragon. The cats moved forwards carefully.

First, they reached the high fence and managed to get over – well, cats are good at fences. Then, inch by inch, they crept closer to the slumbering monster. Almost there, almost there … CRACK. Bells looked down; she had trodden on a large twig, which had snapped loudly. Oh oh, she thought. One of the dragon's eyes opened, first just a little bit, then wider. The cats froze.

The dragon pushed the eggs into the back of the barn, stood up, and growled menacingly, 'I've been waiting for you … for a very long time.'

In a flash, the dragon picked up one of the cat soldiers with a massive outstretched arm and held the scared little thing in the air.

'My dear little Bells, you're all worried and hot.
Let me cool you down in my cooking pot.'

The dragon placed Bells carefully in a very large saucepan, suspended on ropes between trees in the garden. Under the giant saucepan was a large pile of wood ready to be lit. Inside, Bells found herself in some cold water. She found it quite refreshing, until she realised what was going to happen.

Snapper couldn't bear the sight of Bells in trouble. He mewed aggressively and charged towards the dragon, his sword at the ready.

'Cute little Snapper, you're so very brave,
But you'll be taking your courage with you to your grave.'

The dragon's paw swooped over and grabbed Snapper, putting him in the pot next to Bells. Meanwhile, Greystoke was looking around. If she could just tie the spare ropes on the ground round the dragon's neck and devise a quick pulley system, she might be able to strangle the beast. But just as she was formulating her clever plan, the dragon picked her up.

'Greystoke, oh Greystoke, you think you're so smart,
  But you'll taste good in a cat brain tart!'

There was only one of them left. Perch gulped hard. She knew
that the lives of her friends were in her hands. And then the
booming voice was directed at her.

'After centuries this is the end of my search,
  For you must be the cat called Perch.
  The legend says that you are magic,
  But your story to me is nothing but tragic.
  I'll enjoy hearing your moans and groans,
  As I cook you up and chew on your bones.'

The dragon clearly liked its own rhyme, as it started laughing.
Loud, villainous guffaws came bellowing from a wide open
mouth, as its head rocked backwards and forwards.

'Ha, ha, ha, ha, ha … ooh, ooh ooh, ooh … aah, aah, aaah,
aaah …'

Perch saw her one chance, and with all her strength she
threw her sword, aiming at the wobbly bit hanging down at the
back of the dragon's throat. The sword arced through the air,
handle over blade, and stuck right where it was meant to. The
Rhyming Dragon choked and spluttered, and even tried to put
its fingers into its mouth to get the sword out. But its fingers
were too big, and the dragon's head sunk to the ground. With
great effort the dragon softly muttered:

'I can't believe a cat has killed *me*,
  But I'll laugh last, just wait and see.'

And, with its last breath, the dragon let out a small flame from its mouth. The flame lit the rope on the ground and set alight the pile of wood under the cooking pot.

'Oh, this is better,' said Bells from inside the pot. 'It's like a nice warm bath now.'

Perch grabbed a ladder from the barn and some spare rope, and started climbing up the side of the pot.

'Ow, ouch, it's getting too hot now,' shouted Bells. 'Perch, can't you turn the cold on?'

Perch was at the top of the pot. 'Grab this rope,' she yelled. Then, one by one, she pulled her friends out of the pot to safety. They shook the water off their fur. Bells thought she would never want to have a bath again.

Before they could head back to the village there were two things to do. First, they would need proof of the dragon's death. The dragon's head was too big to carry back, so Snapper cut out one of the dragon's eyeballs, which was like a football, and put it in a sack. Second, Bells put the three dragon eggs into the pot of very hot water.

'Those will make nice boiled eggs for someone,' she said.

'More like hard-boiled,' replied Perch.

But Greystoke was doing some calculations. 'How many eggs did you put in the pot?' she asked Bells.

'Three.'

Greystoke was sure she had seen the dragon move four eggs, and found the last one under straw in the very back of the barn. As she approached, sudden wriggling inside the egg startled her, and a small crack appeared in the shell. I can do without any sequels, thought Greystoke, as she grabbed the last egg and popped it in with the others.

And so the victors set off. They had been walking for a few

minutes, but something was niggling Perch. She wasn't sure at first what it was, but knew something wasn't quite right. Why would the dragon choose to sleep half in and half out of an old barn, when the forest provided ample protection? Then it came to her. She rushed back and opened the double-doors to the back section of the barn. Staring right at her were over thirty dirty faces, the lost children huddled together against the cold. They were scared and filthy, but alive.

The four cats were greeted by a vast cheering crowd when they arrived back at the village. Together with the lost children they made their way to the central square, where there was much rejoicing and many tears. Everyone wanted to slap the cats' backs, and Arnold hugged them all. Tommy raced over and gave Perch a sloppy kiss on her nose.

'I told you,' he said. 'I knew you'd save us from the moment I saw you.'

Then Arnold presented the king, who had come from his palace. The king asked Perch to go onto one knee. He placed his sword, a little worryingly, close to her neck, and said: 'Arise, Sir Perchalot.'

It was a great honour to be made a knight although Perch felt that, technically, she should have been made a Dame. The king offered them anything they wanted as a reward, but all

Perch asked for was to be taken back to the field where they had arrived. They were led there and, hand in hand, the cats squelched through the mud until they were swallowed up in a whoosh and found themselves back in Hornsey library. Perch put the book right at the back where nobody would find it, and they slipped past the librarian out into the street.

After such an adventure they couldn't possibly go straight home, so they did what had become their favourite late afternoon treat. They went to the back of the coffee shop, in an alley behind Crouch End High Street, where the kind owner brought them leftover frothy warm milk and some yummy pieces of biscuits and cakes.

That night, lying at the foot of Charlie's bed, Perch purred sweetly as she remembered the moment her pals had come through the book and joined in with her adventure. It felt as if, together with Charlie, they were her family. And if she were asked for any family stories again she would tell the Legend of the Magic Cat.

And there's one thing you can be absolutely positive about. After a day like that, Perch the cat slept very well indeed.

Chapter 3

Operation Perch

One bright summer morning, Perch woke up to the shrill sound of the doorbell ringing. She knew that Charlie wasn't going to get it, as he'd told her that he would be leaving early in the morning. Something about signing books.

Charlie hadn't been in a very good mood over the past few weeks. He had needed another operation on his knee, and hadn't been able to play his beloved cricket for a while. Although the exhilaration of Test Match involvement was in the past, Charlie still loved cricket and supported his country avidly. Recently, however, he'd been experiencing the highs and lows of watching England's batting on the TV.

'When I played we won the Ashes … twice,' he kept muttering under his breath, even though there had been successes since. Perch didn't understand what it meant, but hoped that signing some books would cheer him up.

Perch crawled out of her basket and clambered onto the windowsill to open the door. It was Snapper, who was so excited that he had forgotten about the cat-flap, and Perch could hardly understand what he was saying. While Perch liked to get up slowly and lazily, Snapper was a real morning cat, bouncing out of his basket as soon as the sun rose. This morning, he seemed even more animated than normal.

'You won't believe it, building site, building site, you won't believe it,' Snapper kept repeating in a very excited voice.

'What?' said Perch. 'You're building a kite, that's very nice.'

'No!' said Snapper. 'There's a new building site.'

'Oh, new buildings, I'll see them later,' replied Perch.

'No, no!! A new building site – bricks, ladders, scaffolding, all brilliant for climbing and playing.'

'I see,' said Perch, relieved that she understood Snapper. 'I would love to come and play with you at the new building site.'

Snapper told Perch where the site was, and they agreed a time to meet. He said that Bells would be there too. Perch had noticed over recent weeks that Snapper and Bells were often touching paws, and seemed to be doing lots of things together.

Once, Perch had seen them having a  kiss on the lips in a doorway – they were giggling as their whiskers tickled each other. The two seemed to be more than just cat-friends. Perch was pleased for them both, although she missed the special time with her buddy Bells.

·ᴥ·

About an hour later Perch was at the building site. It was a fifteen-minute walk from her house, through the centre of Crouch End with all its shops, cafes and restaurants. Perch shuddered as she walked past the pet shop, quickening her step with fear that Peter might reach out and grab her.

The building site was part of the sports club in Coolhurst Road, where they were building more tennis courts and a new clubhouse. It was lunchtime, so the builders weren't there, and the site was deserted. The new buildings were half-built, with steel poles coming out of the floors, and there were lots of wooden beams, which were great for getting your claws into. They looked like giant unfinished Lego toys.

It was the ground area of the new tennis courts that Perch most liked the look of. The surface was very flat and beautifully smooth, and Perch imagined skidding and sliding across it. There were planks of wood laid down all the way around the court, and Perch thought it would make a great running track. As she was contemplating all the exciting possibilities, Snapper and Bells arrived. Snapper was stroking Bells' ear, and they seemed to be in good spirits.

'You're a bit late,' said Perch, a little irritated. 'I've been here for ages.'

'I'm really sorry,' replied Snapper. 'But we couldn't help it.'

'Why, what were you two *love-cats* up to?' Perch wished she hadn't said the word love-cats the moment it had come out of her mouth.

Bells and Snapper stared straight at Perch, somewhat taken aback.

'We were … er … er … were …' Snapper was muttering. He was unable to finish, so Bells came in with a fib.

'We were at Stationer's Park, trying out the new Superslide if you must know – though, I'm not sure that it's any of your business.'

Perch didn't think the conversation was going very well, and wondered whether maybe she was a little jealous. She didn't feel like an argument, so she tried to lighten the atmosphere.

'Oh, I've heard about that new Superslide, with its big bumps and tunnel. It sounds terrific.'

'Yeah, yeah, it was, really fast,' joined in Snapper

enthusiastically. 'And Bells loved it too.' Bells nodded, and Perch was glad. She was about to say something but Snapper was off, darting over to the nearest building, bounding up the beams and over poles up to the highest point. Then he leapt in the air and landed on the top of the wall of the next building. A ladder was lying from that wall over to another one, and Snapper raced across it, two rungs at a time. He was obviously very, very happy. Perch looked at Bells, and they smiled at each other, knowingly.

'I'm going to have a go on this bit on the ground,' said Perch, and she walked over to the nearest plank on the side of the flat area.

'Me too,' said Bells.

'Now, please be careful, Bells,' said Perch with concern. 'You know how you can be a little … a little … unlucky.' She hadn't wanted to say *clumsy*, as she didn't want to upset Bells. And they had already had one sticky moment today.

'I'll be fine,' said Bells, and she tore off after Perch. They had a great time racing around the planks, chasing each other, and after four laps they were exhausted. Bells had been a little distracted by the dust messing up her beautifully groomed fur, and had hardly noticed when she had knocked something over.

'I'm going to do a bit of skating,' said Perch.

'Are you sure?' Bells wondered. 'It may not be safe, haven't you seen the …'

But Bells was too late, as Perch had jumped into the middle of the smooth flat area, with a big grin. But Perch didn't slide at all, and the grin was soon off her lovely face. First Perch just looked a bit surprised, as she shouted to Bells about how sticky it was. But then Perch realised she could hardly move her paws. With great effort she managed to slowly pull free out of the

35

ground and onto a plank, but her back right paw was completely stuck. Surprise turned to worry.

'Bells, I'm stuck,' said the voice of a scared cat.

'You didn't let me finish my sentence before,' said Bells anxiously. 'Didn't you see the sign?'

'No, what sign?'

'That one there,' said Bells, as she pointed to where the sign had been. But it had fallen onto its side. 'Oh, I think I might have knocked it over. Sorry.'

'Well, what did it say?' asked Perch.

'It said … *Beware – Wet Cement* '.

Perch gulped hard.

The clock in Crouch End chimed that it was two in the afternoon. Perch reckoned that the builders must have laid the cement just before lunchtime. Cement dries fast, so there was probably only about ten minutes before her leg would be completely fixed in the hard ground. She remembered Charlie saying that builders have long lunches, so she couldn't rely on the builders helping her.

Snapper was startled as he heard Perch screaming for help. In just a few bounds he was down by Bells' side, and together they tried to pull Perch out. The two cats yanked as hard as they could, but the leg wouldn't budge, and they had to be careful not to fall in themselves.

'You really are in a bit of a fix,' smirked Snapper, pleased with his own pun. 'We'll have to get some help.'

'Good idea' said Perch. 'You go, and Bells can stay and keep me company.'

Snapper took two steps, but then stopped in his tracks. He sniffed the air. Snapper could sense danger and he knew that something wasn't right. He glanced back at Perch and Bells, who were watching and wondering what was wrong.

Then they heard the first growl. It came from the far corner of the building site, and made all the cats shiver. They looked over and saw the meanest white bulldog they had ever set eyes on. More nasty loud barks came from beside the half-built clubhouse where Snapper had been playing. There were two more bulldogs, with black and white patches, baring their teeth at the cats.

As if that wasn't bad enough, Perch then heard a different kind of yowl. It was a quieter sound, but still unpleasant and coming from a little nearer. On the other side of the cats were two large poodles, who did not look happy at all. The cats looked at each other, terrified. They were surrounded.

'You've got to get me out of here,' said Perch desperately. 'Be quick,

and don't worry too much about those two, they're just poodles.'

'Oh dear, dear, dear,' said Bells.

'What is it?' said Snapper, who couldn't imagine what else could be the matter.

'That poodle on the right, she's pregnant,' said Bells. 'They're always hungry, and they'll eat anything.'

The poodles were walking menacingly towards the cats. They were now very close, and Perch strained to hear what they were after.

'I want meat,' said the heavily pregnant girl poodle to the boy poodle, as she stared at Perch.

'Whatever you want,' the boy poodle responded.

'Hold on, actually I want pickled cucumbers. No, as you were … meat.'

The boy poodle got the message and moved forwards towards Perch. He was about to ask her if she knew where the nearest butcher was, when he noticed the bulldogs. The standard poodles hated the bulldogs because they teased them about their curly black fur. The disagreements often ended in nasty scraps. The boy poodle took a step forwards towards Perch. He wanted to tell her that he would help the cats.

Unfortunately though, Snapper thought the poodle was about to attack Bells and Perch. Believing that he had little time, he grabbed a plank of wood from the ground and stood between the poodle and his trapped friends. The animals were glaring at each other, and it was only Bells who noticed that the plank had been supporting a pile of shelves, on the top of which was a heavy-looking bucket. The shelves wobbled and the bucket crashed onto the poodle's head. He fell to the ground, knocked out. The girl poodle looked Snapper in the eyes, as if to say, "I will never forget your face," and then licked her partner sadly to try and rouse him.

The bulldogs barked at each other and turned and went off.

They could tell that the cats would be trouble and they needed assistance.

'We've got to be very fast,' said Snapper. 'They'll be back soon with all their bulldog friends.'

'What, a whole group of them?' said Bells.

'Yes,' replied Snapper. 'But you don't call it a group of dogs – it's a … a … herd of dogs.'

'A herd of *cows*, you fool,' came in Bells. It's a … a … school of dogs.'

'A school is for bees,' said Snapper angrily. He didn't like being wrong. 'Isn't it a colony of dogs?'

Perch couldn't believe what she was hearing. 'Guys,' she cried, 'we're in a bit of a hurry, and anyway it's a …'

She didn't get to finish her sentence, because a calm velvety voice interrupted. It was a voice they hadn't heard before, but the sort of voice that you want to hear when you need help. It was gentle, strong, and wise. It was also the voice of an animal that had been around for many years.

'I can clear things up, my dear pets,' said the voice. 'It's a school of fish, a swarm of bees, a colony of ants and, my favourite, a pod of dolphins. And it's a pack of dogs.'

'Isn't it a pack of cards?' asked Bells, who didn't quite get it at all.

'Oh, do be quiet, Bells,' said Perch. 'And who are you?'

'The name's Alfred,' replied the old dog. 'And I think we'd better hurry – the bulldogs will be back soon.'

Alfred was a shaggy golden-coloured labrador. He had a friendly, kind manner, and he soon got to work. He grabbed a bucket of water and tipped it into the cement around Perch's paw. He had to do everything slowly because of his age, and his movements were a bit lumbering. Then he picked up a spade and used it to force some of the wetter cement away from Perch. Finally he opened his mouth as if to take a bite out of Perch's paw.

'Hey, what are you doing?' asked Bells quickly.

'Don't worry, my friend,' said Alfred. 'I haven't got any teeth.'

So Alfred put his slobbery mouth around Perch's leg and sucked and pulled. The leg came out with a pop, and was all red and bruised.

'Thank you so much,' said a relieved Perch. 'But I can't move it.'

'Looks broken to me,' said Alfred wisely. 'We need to get you to hospital.'

'But I can't walk.'

Luckily Alfred seemed to have an answer for everything. With his tail he pointed to his back.

'Hop on.'

So they moved off and, after a short while, Perch became sleepy. The draining experience with the cement had taken its toll, and the rocking motion of Alfred's walk was making her so tired. As Perch closed her eyes, all Alfred could hear was one word being quietly repeated.

'Charlie … Charlie … Charl … Cha …'

At St Catherine's Hospital for Sick Cats, Perch was taken straight up to the Florence Nightingale ward. Only one animal was allowed to go with her, and she chose Alfred. Normally dogs weren't allowed into the cat hospital – for obvious reasons – but when the nurse saw the exhausted-looking Alfred, she was worried that he might need a bed himself. Bells and Snapper had to wait outside, anxiously biting their finger-claws.

'Don't I get my own room?' asked Perch gently, as she realised she was sharing a room with three other ill cats.

'This isn't a private hospital,' replied the nurse softly.

The nurse realised that Perch was anxious, so she continued, 'Please don't worry, we'll look after you very well. Just rest on the bed here.'

So Perch lay down on the bed and the kind-looking nurse took her temperature. Then the nurse held Perch's wrist.

'It's my leg that hurts,' said Perch, trying to be helpful.

'I'm taking your pulse,' said the nurse. 'That's your heartbeat – now relax and the doctor will be along soon.'

Normally in hospitals "soon" can mean quite a long wait, but Perch was fortunate and shortly the doctor arrived. He was a suave, confident man, who was well-dressed and clean-cut. And he had a perfectly combed side-parting in his brown hair. The doctor sat down on the side of the bed and looked at her.

'My name's Dr Hubens. I'm the on-call surgeon. What seems to be the problem?' He spoke beautifully, Oxford English, though he seemed in a hurry.

Perch pointed to her painful, swollen right lower leg, and started to explain what had happened with the cement and the dogs.

'I don't need to know all that,' interrupted Dr Hubens rudely. 'I'm off to the theatre in ten minutes. Just show me exactly where it hurts.' Perch put her finger on the spot, and the doctor prodded around, not very delicately.

'OW!' yelled Perch. 'Can't you be a bit more careful?!'

The doctor didn't seem to be paying much attention. He looked at Perch's chart at the end of her bed, then picked up the

X-ray that Perch had been sent for earlier. He held it up to the light.

'Fractured fibula. No need for a CAT-scan. It's nothing serious. We'll put you in a cast for three months and you'll be fine.'

'Are you sure?' asked Perch. 'Isn't there … anything else that could be done?'

Dr Hubens smirked. 'I think I know what's best for you, my dear. If you've got any questions just ask the nurse. Or the junior doctor over there.'

Perch looked over at the

young doctor who Hubens had pointed to. He had deep-set eyes and was wandering around the ward with hunched shoulders.

'He looks a bit mean, what's his name?' said Perch.

'Oh, don't worry about him. Crippen's a harmless fellow – good doctor though. I'm rather busy, I'll see you later.' And, with that, Dr Hubens started to walk off.

But everyone seemed to have forgotten about Alfred, who was lying on the floor on the other side of the bed, listening carefully to everything. Alfred had clearly heard enough, and stood up.

'Just you wait a minute,' Alfred announced, with such authority that the doctor stopped and turned around. He was also rather surprised to hear a dog's voice in the hospital. 'Come back,' Alfred continued. 'We need to have a little talk.' Dr

Hubens had to obey words spoken with such calm seriousness.

'When you were learning to be a doctor, didn't they teach you how important it is to communicate with your patients, to speak to them nicely? And to treat them well?'

'Not really,' Hubens replied, a bit embarrassed. 'They just taught us the facts, the science. How the body works, what happens when things go wrong. Made us learn things by heart – then exams, exams, and more exams.' The doctor looked sad about it.

'Nothing about listening to your patients and respecting what they want?' asked Alfred gently.

'No.'

'Well, I'm going to try and help,' continued Alfred. 'Have you ever heard of the great philosophers?'

'No,' said Hubens. 'Who are they?'

'Well, philosophers are great thinkers, and in history there have been some really clever thinkers.'

Dr Hubens settled down. He was interested and listened attentively. Perch also sat right up. She loved hearing Alfred take control.

'In different times there have been different philosophers,' continued Alfred. 'For example, there were the medieval philosophers.'

Perch jumped in. 'I've been to the medieval times – I killed a dragon!' Dr Hubens grinned and asked Alfred to carry on.

'I'm going to tell you about some really special thinkers, called the cat philosophers.'

Hubens was intrigued. 'Weren't there any dog philosophers?' he asked.

Alfred didn't bother to answer because he was in full flow. 'The first great cat philosopher lived in Greek times and was called SoCates. He was a wise, old mog. He didn't write anything down but spent all his time speaking to other cats in the streets. SoCates famously said that an unexamined cat's life is not worth living.'

'What does that mean?' asked Dr Hubens.

'It means that it's always good to think about what you say and do, rather than just doing things because you're told to.' Hubens thought about this.

'The next philosopher I want to tell you about lived about four hundred years ago in France. Her name was Renee DesCates. When she was a kitten she got trapped in an oven.'

'Was it turned on?' asked Perch.

'Luckily not,' replied Alfred. 'But DesCates was in the oven a long time and when she came out she suddenly announced, "I think, therefore I am!" and everyone thought she was brilliant.' So did Hubens.

Alfred carried on. 'But now I want to get to the most important one of all, the grandfather of all the cat philosophers.'

'Who's that?' asked the doctor.

'The great German philosopher Immanuel Kat. He wrote lots and lots of books that were so clever that most people couldn't understand them. But he came up with one idea that is very important to Perch's broken leg. He called it his "categorical imperative".'

'His whatty whatty?' said a perplexed Dr Hubens.

'Immanuel Kat said that we shouldn't use other cats just to help us get what we want, and we should treat all other cats with respect.'

Alfred was a wonderful teacher, and he had both Perch and Dr Hubens eating out of the palms of his paws. Hubens was all ears, and enjoying the learning.

'I think I'm beginning to understand,' said the eager doctor. 'By not asking Perch what she would like I haven't been respecting her fully.'

'That's right.' Alfred was pleased that his teaching was working well. 'Are there any other choices for Perch?' he asked the doctor.

'Well, yes,' said Dr Hubens. 'She could have an operation, and then be in a cast for only one month.'

Perch's eyes lit up. She hated the idea of three months in the cast and didn't mind the thought of an operation at all. Dr Hubens thanked Alfred for all his wisdom, and promised to be a more friendly doctor. Hubens explained everything to Perch, and began wheeling the bed down to the operating theatre.

* * *

It was the evening after the operation and they were all gathered around Perch's hospital bed. Snapper and Bells were drawing on Perch's hard white plaster of Paris. Alfred and Dr Hubens were excitedly discussing the Russian philosophers, all animated and waving paws. Perch was comfortably lying in the bed, enjoying all the love around her. Then in walked Charlie, one of his large hands holding both his motorcycle helmet and a big bunch of flowers – he was using the other hand to repeatedly throw a cricket ball gently up in the air and catch it. He looked a lot happier after signing some books.

Perch noticed that Greystoke, whose blue-grey fur looked incredibly smart, had something to say.

'We couldn't go to the coffee shop,' Greystoke announced, as she quickly wrote some numbers and letters on Perch's leg.

IF $2x + y = 12$, AND $y = 6$, WHAT IS x ?

'So I've brought the coffee shop to you.'

And, with that, Greystoke placed on the table a cardboard tray full of cups of frothy milk and milk chocolate bars. They took a cup each and held it up. Perch was about to make a toast, but then indicated to Alfred that he should do it.

'When you're ill,' said the wise old dog, 'you really find out who your friends are. So the toast is "Friends together – in sickness and in health".'

'In sickness and in health,' they all repeated.

Perch was trying to take a sip, but it felt all wrong. Her lips should have been wet from the milk, but they felt dry. And she was coughing and choking. Perch had an image of everyone around her, but her eyes felt as if they were closed. So she tried to open them. At first everything looked fuzzy and blurred, and then she began to make out shapes in the room.

'You're alright, my love,' said a comforting voice. 'You're safe now, back at home in my bed.'

Perch opened her eyes and saw Charlie sitting in front of her on the bed, caressing her gently. She was very pleased to see him.

'Something strange happened,' Charlie continued. 'I was signing some books, and the last one was given to me by a tall man. I couldn't see his face but his hat looked familiar. I opened the book to sign my autograph, and looked up to ask him if there was anything special he wanted me to write. But he had left, and I noticed he had written one word in the book. "Home." I sensed something was wrong and came straight back.

Charlie pointed to the cats and dog in the room. 'All this lot were outside the front door. You were unconscious, and the old dog looked like he was going to pass out too. I noticed your leg and took you straight to the vet, who had to operate.'

Perch looked around her, still piecing the bits together. It had happened, but not quite as she had imagined in her dream.

'Seems like your friends saved you. They were so concerned that I let them come in.' Charlie leant in a bit closer. 'It's good to have my soulmate back,' he whispered.

Charlie popped out to get some milk and Bells jumped in, eager to apologise for knocking over the sign.

'It was an accident,' she explained to the patient.

'I know,' replied Perch. She leant over and gave Bells a big hug, and told Bells how it wasn't her fault at all. Bells felt much better, and drew a smiley face on Perch's hard white leg cast.

As all this was happening, in another part of town an angry Mummy poodle gave birth to a puppy, to whom she would tell the story about what happened to her poor Daddy at the building site.

But the cats were unaware of all of this, and thrilled that things had worked out alright. Charlie, who knew a thing or two about operations, returned with the milk, and explained that Perch needed her rest. And there's one thing you can bet your bottom dollar on. That night, even with her leg in a cast, love shone through, and Perch the cat slept very well indeed.

Chapter 4

The Curse of Crazybones

It was a Sunday in early autumn when Perch woke up with a spring in her step. Although it was only eight in the morning, Perch jumped perkily out of her basket and opened the curtains in the lounge. She could sense the chill in the air, but outside the garden was lit up by hazy sunshine streaming down from a light blue sky.

She popped through the cat-flap and went over to the pond to check on her fish-friends. They were all there, safe and sound, and happy for their morning feed. Perch sniffed the air and, making her way back to the house, thought what a beautiful day it would be for a walk in Kenwood. Perch liked going for countryside walks with Charlie, but on his last few London trips Charlie had been too busy with school children at the cricket nets in Highgate Woods. So, wanting company and feeling bold, Perch dropped in on Snapper. She told him of her plans, and he was more than happy to join her.

Now, Kenwood is part of Hampstead Heath, a big park full of open fields, swimming ponds, and deep, dark woods. But there is one particular area of woods that people, and especially cats, have tended to stay away from. This part of the woods, tucked behind the largest pond, has been well known to local people for some time, but not for good reasons. The woods here are believed to be haunted.

Over the years, many cats have gone missing in these woods, never to be seen again, so much so that the park keeper has put up a big, white sign with red capital letters saying, *"CATS – BEWARE"*. On a weekend you would hardly ever see people

walking in the "haunted woods", and you certainly would never see any cats there.

Dear old Perch and Snapper, though, had no idea whatsoever about any of this. Happy as pie they mooched past the entrance to Kenwood House, a big old white building with lots of paintings inside. Perch liked to pop in at the end of a walk to get warm, and to look at the beautiful pictures.

'Let's get going,' said Snapper excitedly, bouncing around as ever. Perch thought Snapper looked particularly handsome, his dark brown Burmese fur beautifully groomed.

So the two cats set off merrily down the pebbled paths, and after a few minutes

were heading straight towards the haunted woods. Charlie had never taken Perch to this part of Hampstead Heath, so there was no reason why she, or indeed Snapper, would have known anything about its history. Chatting away to each other they completely missed the warning sign, and before they knew it they were right in the heart of the part of the woods which most people, and almost all cats, did their very best to avoid.

All of a sudden, Perch and Snapper stopped speaking to one another. The beautiful autumn sunshine had disappeared and the sky had turned very dark. And it felt cold – the sort of chill that gets you deep inside and makes you shudder. Perch inched closer to Snapper, hoping that he would do likewise. He did, and Perch felt comforted. She also felt a tingle run down her spine as her fur brushed against his, and it wasn't because of the cold or dark.

'I don't like this,' said Perch. 'Let's go back.'

Snapper held tight onto Perch's paw. 'Yes, I think that's a good idea,' he replied and admitted, quietly to himself, that even *he* felt a little scared.

Snapper turned around to retrace their steps. But behind them were several paths, and neither of the cats could remember which path they had come down.

Just as they were doing "eeney-meany-miney-mo" to pick a path, a deep, thick mist seemed to fill the air, swirling around with the wind. It was difficult to see much, but all around them appeared strange cat-like shapes hovering above the ground and moving between the trees. The cat shapes, all different in size, were silent and staring, with their arms held out in front of them. It was like they were drawn in outline only, as if they were half real and – Perch could hardly think it – half spirit.

'They look like … g … g … ghosts,' said a scared Perch.

51

'Or … zombies,' replied Snapper. They turned and looked at each other and, for the first time ever, Perch saw fear in Snapper's eyes. Snapper, of course, tried to hide it, and to take control.

'Run!' he tried to shout. But it came out quietly and, most horribly, they couldn't. Their legs would only move very, very slowly. They were trapped in the misty spell of the haunted woods.

As the two cats tried desperately to urge their legs forwards, a whooshing sound could be heard high in the trees. They looked up and saw a much darker and bigger cloud of greyness, most definitely in the shape of a giant Persian cat. Snapper was speechless, staring at the large ghost cat in the sky, with his mouth wide open.

As luck would have it though, Perch was standing next to a prickly holly bush. It took her a few moments, but eventually she managed to brush her zombified body up against one of the prickles. It did exactly what she had hoped for, it shocked her partly out of the zombification and allowed her to speak slowly.

'Who … are … you?' she asked the cloud of ghost cat.

'The name's Bohhhnes,' boomed the voice from the trees.

'What is … happening … to us?' Every word was hard work for Perch to get out.

'You will be my next zombie cats,' continued Bones.

'What does *that* mean?' said a very anxious Perch.

'It means that you will live under my spell in these woods. Forever.'

'Forever? But that's a very long time.'

'Forever! Yes!' The ghost seemed angry, but also a bit miserable. 'That is my curse.'

Perch could sense the sadness, and also the gentleness, in the voice. So she carried on in the kindest voice she could find. 'What happened to you?'

'Why should I tell *you*?' came a less booming reply.

'Because ... maybe I can help,' answered Perch.

'Why would you care about a ghost like me?'

Perch took her time. 'Because I care about *all* my fellow cats,' she said, 'no matter who they are ... or what has happened to them.'

There was a deep sigh from the cloud, and then Bones said, quietly, 'Very well.'

And he told them his story.

And it went something like this.

Just over one hundred years ago, in late Victorian times, there lived a nasty man called Mr Simpson. Things were rather different in those days – there were no cars, and people used horses and carriages to get around. There was no central heating, and the air was full of smoke from the fires in people's homes and from the factory chimneys. The streets were filthy with rotting food, and people were worried about getting ill from something called the plague, which they thought you caught from rats.

So, Mr Simpson bought a cat to get rid of all the rats in the cellar of his small house near the river Thames in London. The cat was called Bones, but he didn't like catching rats much.

'Do your job!' Mr Simpson used to scream at Bones, as he

kicked the cat down into the dark cellar. 'Don't come back up until you've got a rat in your mouth!'

The neighbours could hear Mr Simpson shouting and the cellar door slamming shut. They felt sorry for Bones, who got his name partly because he loved nothing more than to suck the leftover fish bones in the streets, and partly because mean Mr Simpson never fed him anything, so he was just skin and bones. In spite of this, Bones was a loyal cat, who looked after his owner.

One cold winter evening, just before Christmas, there was a heavy smog in the air. A smog is a mixture of smoke and fog, and on that day it was *so* thick that you couldn't see your hand held out in front of your face. Mr Simpson and Bones were walking down by the river, hurrying to get home before nightfall, when Mr Simpson tripped on a brick lying on the path. He had just been in the pub, drinking too much beer, and was already a bit wobbly on his feet. Bones, trying his best to help, held out his paw to save Mr Simpson, but he couldn't stop his drunken owner from falling into the freezing water and drowning. A nearby policeman heard the splash and ran over, just in time to hear Mr

Simpson's last cries from the water of 'Bones … Bones.'

The policeman held the cat responsible for the murder of his cruel master, and locked him up.

As the local people knew how nasty Mr Simpson was to his cat, they couldn't believe that the death was an accident, even though Bones pleaded his innocence until he was Persian blue in the face. Bones was sent to prison and was sentenced to death by hanging. One of the newspapers, *The London Times*, nicknamed him "Crazybones", and wrote about him being a dangerous and savage killer cat.

On the day of the hanging, a large crowd gathered in Noose Square. As Crazybones was about to be hanged by the scruff of his neck, the executioner appeared to wait, as if expecting the cat to come out with some last words. Crazybones looked out at the crowd, drew a deep breath in, and a terrifying meow filled the air. Out of the menacing sound people swore they heard the words:

'I am innocent – it is all of you who are guilty. My blood will forever be on your hands.'

Men and women in the crowd shivered as the cat stared at them, one by one.

'I will never rest,' continued Crazybones in his own thoughts, 'but instead will haunt the woods on Hampstead Heath, where I used to walk with my master on the weekends, and will turn each cat who dares to enter my sacred place into …. a zombie.' And, with that, the executioner opened the trapdoor and Crazybones had his last breath.

And, for one hundred years, Crazybones had been doing exactly what he had promised.

Perch and Snapper were dumbfounded, and they stared in disbelief at the ghost cat as he finished telling them his tale.

'But that's the saddest story I've ever heard,' said Perch.

'It's the story of my life,' came the reply from above. 'I am innocent.'

'But it's not fair,' said Perch. Snapper tried to join in but he couldn't manage to speak.

'I know,' said Crazybones. 'Life is not always fair.'

Perch was thinking carefully. She had many wonderful qualities for a cat. She was kind, honest, thoughtful, caring, and a wonderful friend. But she also had a real sense of justice. She couldn't bear it when things didn't turn out fair. So she asked a simple question.

'Is there anything we can do to help?'

Crazybones thought about it. 'You want to help me?' he enquired.

'I do,' said Perch very definitely. 'All this wrong must be put right.' Snapper was trying to nod his head but it was too hard work.

After a while Crazybones' eyes seemed to light up a little, and he had an idea.

'There is something,' he said. 'It's the only chance. There was a little boy, about seven or eight years old, whose name was … Robert …. Robert …' Crazybones was thinking really hard, trying desperately to remember. Eventually he continued.

'His last name was … Snorter … no, no, no … Daughter … no, no … Porter, yes Porter. Robert Porter. But everyone called him Robbie, Robbie Porter. He was a lovely little lad, Robbie.

His mum and dad had died from the plague, and he lived with his Aunty Doris in the house next to Mr Simpson, right by the river. He loved stroking me and was always hanging around our house. But he had to run away whenever Mr Simpson saw him, as Mr Simpson didn't like children.'

'He was really horrible, that Mr Simpson,' said Perch.

'Yes, he was, but he was also my owner,' answered Crazybones, 'so I looked out for him. It's important to respect your owner.' Perch thought about how much she adored Charlie, and nodded.

'Robbie Porter,' continued Crazybones, 'was sitting with his back to a wall by the river the day that Mr Simpson fell in. He saw everything, and knew it wasn't my fault. He tried to tell the policeman, but the policeman wouldn't listen because Robbie was just a young lad. Robbie cried when they took me away.'

'That's all very interesting,' said Perch. 'But why is it important to us, now?'

'Be patient,' said Crazybones, 'I've had to be for the last hundred years. Robbie was always writing in a little book, his diary, and he was writing just when it all happened. If we could find Robbie's diary, it could be the evidence that shows that I was not guilty, that I didn't push Mr Simpson into the river.'

Perch thought. 'But that's a long, long time ago. What are we supposed to do?'

Crazybones was quick to answer. 'You must go to Robbie's old house and search for the diary. He lived at number 10 Memory Lane, right by the river near Blackfriars Bridge.'

'But I can hardly move,' said Perch. 'And Snapper can't move at all.'

'This will help,' said Crazybones, as his ghost mouth blew a little bit of the mist away from the cats on the ground. They felt a little better, and Snapper was finally able to move his body. 'But beware,' continued Crazybones, 'the spell has been cast and, although it has eased a little for now, you will still turn into complete zombies within twenty-four hours. Unless, unless, you are able to prove me innocent and free me from the curse.'

Perch and Snapper looked at each other with alarm. 'We'll do our best,' said Perch, and they set off.

Progress was very slow, every movement demanding a lot of effort, and it took them an hour just to get out of Hampstead Heath. They walked as if they were almost zombies, with their front paws out in front of them. Snapper was very, very quiet, and Perch began to get worried.

'Are you OK, Snapper?' she asked.

Snapper looked down at his paws on the ground. 'You won't tell anyone that I was scared, will you?'

'Of course not,' Perch replied.

'Especially Bells,' added Snapper.

'Especially Bells.'

'And you won't tell anyone that I couldn't move or save you?'

'Absolutely not,' said Perch. 'Mum's the word.'

After that Snapper seemed to perk up a bit and they got on with their journey. They meandered down the back streets towards the City of London and, six hours later, arrived at Memory Lane. Number ten was a run-down old house by the river, with some windows broken and others with boards over them. It didn't look like anybody had been living in it for years. It was the evening by now, and the darkness seemed to make things even worse. The cats went up to the front door. Snapper had little energy left, so Perch tried to knock but, as she did, her paw just pushed the door open. It creaked scarily.

Perch went in first and tried the light switch but it didn't work. She did find a candle on the floor, though, which she lit and they both walked carefully further into the house. Cobwebs and dust were everywhere, and there was a stale, unpleasant smell.

'I don't like it,' said Snapper.

'Me neither,' said Perch. 'But we've got to look around, or you know what will become of us.'

First, they went through what looked like the lounge, where there was an armchair and a blanket and even an old telly. But no book, no diary. Then they walked through the kitchen, where there were some plates in the sink. But no book. Nothing in the bathroom or bedroom either. Finally they went into a small room that looked like a study, as it had a desk and an old telephone.

'Let's look in the desk,' said Perch.

'OK,' said Snapper. 'You go ahead and I'll watch out.'

Perch opened a couple of drawers but found nothing. With her heart low she opened the last drawer and, inside, she saw a small, old book, with a dark red cover. On the front it said, "Diary, Robbie Porter, 1905". Perch opened it up and went straight to the entry for the day that Mr Simpson died, December the fifth. She brushed off some dust with her paw and blew off the rest, which made Snapper cough. She read all that Robbie had written, and when she came to the end Perch was desperate to share it with Snapper.

'Listen to this,' said Perch. 'In the diary Robbie wrote:

"I saw Bones try to save Mr Simspon, but the policeman

didn't care. The policeman told me to be quiet and took Bones away, so it looked like he had solved the crime. I yelled and yelled, and cried and cried. But nobody listened. It was all wrong".'

Snapper gasped and was about to speak, when they both heard something they didn't like, the sound of floorboards creaking. Then the study door slowly opened. The cats grabbed each other in fear.

The voice they heard was very old and slow. 'Can … I … help … you?' it asked. Perch held up her candle and the two cats saw the oldest man they had ever seen.

'Who are you?' questioned Perch.

'I was about to ask you the same thing,' the old man continued. 'But I might as well start. My name is Mr Robert Porter, and you're in my house, the same house I've lived in all my life.'

'You're Robbie Porter,' said Perch. 'Then you must know all about Crazybones.'

'Yes, I am Robbie Porter,' replied the old man, 'but nobody has called me Robbie since I was a lad, which was a long time ago. I'm 112 years old, you know.'

'That *is* old,' said Perch.

'And yes,' continued Robbie, 'I remember all about Crazybones, though his real name was Bones. I loved that cat with all my heart, and what happened to him was terrible. I couldn't bear to go to the hanging. The unfairness of it all has lived with me through my life. Never a day goes by when I don't think about dear old Bones.'

Perch and Snapper looked at each other, and then Perch told Robbie the whole story of the curse of Crazybones; how the ghost cat still lived in Hampstead Heath, and how lots of other cats had been turned into zombies. And, most importantly, how it could all be put right if they could prove that Crazybones was innocent.

'You must take my diary to the City of London police museum,' said Robbie, once Perch was finished. 'It's near here and should still be open. That's where they have the file of Crazybones' case, and that's how you can prove he was innocent. Go, go now, before it is too late.'

'Won't you come with?' asked Perch.

'I'm too old,' said Robbie. 'Anyway, your story has completed my life. Now I know that Crazybones will be OK, I can rest in peace.'

And, with that, Robbie went and sat quietly in the armchair, breathed deeply, and closed his eyes. There was a sweet smile on Robbie's face and Perch went over and licked him goodbye.

It was all a bit easier at the police museum than they had imagined. The curator, who was a police sergeant, knew all about the famous story of Crazybones, even though it was a long time ago. He got out the file from a drawer and carefully read Robbie Porter's diary. The evidence in the diary was clearly all that was needed, and the sergeant immediately phoned up *The London Times* newspaper.

When the cats left the police museum it was very late, and it took them the whole night to get back to Kenwood. They had picked up the early morning newspaper on the way, and on the front page was the perfect headline. It said, quite simply, "*Crazybones is Innocent*". By the time they reached the haunted woods they could hardly move their bodies at all, as it was nearly the hour of full zombification.

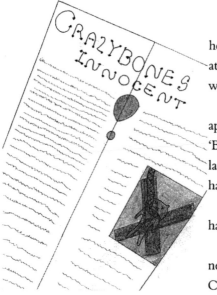

Perch mustered all her effort and shouted up at the trees, 'Crazybones, we're here ... we're back.'

The ghost cat appeared high up in trees. 'But I fear you are too late,' he called back. 'You have run out of time.'

'No!' said Perch. 'We have the evidence. Look.'

Perch held up the newspaper for Crazybones to see, and a broad, gentle smile appeared on the ghost cat's face. Perch quickly told Cazybones the whole adventure, and how they had met his old friend Robbie Porter.

'I am free,' Crazybones answered. 'You have proved my innocence, and the curse is lifted. Now I, too, can rest in peace.'

A warm wind seemed to fill the air and the ghost cat swirled around up in the trees. Perch and Snapper found that they could move their limbs again, and lots of other cats were running out from the woods, freed from being zombies.

Perch looked up again – she could just make out Crazybones' smiling face being blown by the wind into the sky.

'We'll never forget you, Crazybones,' she shouted. 'We love you.'

Perch listened carefully and heard a wispy last few words from on high.

'The name's ... Bohhhnes ...'

And with that, he was gone.

'So you won't tell anybody that I was scared?' checked Snapper again as they walked to the coffee shop.

'Of course not,' said Perch.

'Or that I couldn't move my limbs, or got frightened at the old man's house?'

'Not a word,' said Perch.

Out the back of the coffee shop, Greystoke and Alfred couldn't quite believe the amazing story and Greystoke suggested all kinds of clever ways to break a zombie spell. Bells listened to everything very carefully, but said little and didn't even drink her frothy milk. Perch didn't notice, however, because she was rather distracted. She was thinking about what a remarkable day she had had. Dangerous, scary, but amazing. And as she lay in her basket that night, exhausted, she found it surprisingly hard to nod off. Eventually, though, she found something that helped her. It was the comforting thought of Snapper's paws on hers that allowed Perch the cat to fall into a deep, restful sleep.

Chapter 5

The Catlas Mountains

Perch had been awake for a while when she first heard Charlie's footsteps upstairs. Over the past few weeks, Charlie had been encouraging Perch not to sleep in too late. Instead, he suggested that she come up to his bedroom early in the morning, give him a lick on the nose and snuggle up in the thick covers. It had been working well, but on this particular morning Perch didn't want to get out of her golden basket at all.

It was that time at the end of October, when it wasn't quite autumn and it wasn't yet winter. But it felt like winter. The wind howled outside, and Perch could feel a draft of cold air spreading through Charlie's old house. She buried herself deep in her blankets, and waited for the central heating to come on. As her mind drifted and she dozed in and out of sleep, Perch wasn't sure whether she was dreaming or not …

'Are you alright?' asked Charlie as he leapt down the stairs, two at a time. He seemed to be in rather a good mood.

'Sure,' said Perch, though it didn't sound like she was so sure.

'Don't you want to get up for some breakfast?' Charlie added.

'In a minute,' replied Perch, though a minute later she still hadn't moved from her cosy spot.

'I've got some news to tell you,' said Charlie. 'Well, more of a surprise really.' Perch's eyes widened, and she stepped out of the basket. She liked surprises.

'What is it?' she asked, pretending not to be too interested but deep down she was intrigued. 'Have you got a present for me?'

'No – not that,' answered Charlie.

'Am I having double-cream for breakfast?'

'No,' replied Charlie. 'You know that's not good for you. And it's more exciting than that.'

More exciting, thought Perch. No, it couldn't be the impossible. It couldn't be what her heart yearned for more than anything. What she dreamt about. She looked up with a kitten's love in her eyes, and couldn't stop herself asking.

'Have you found my parents?'

''Oh, no … sorry, not that,' said Charlie quietly, realising he had raised Perch's hopes by mistake.

'Then what?' questioned Perch.

Charlie went over and gave Perch a gentle stroke, and lifted her up. He knew when a cat needed a cuddle. 'We're going on holiday,' he said as he looked straight into her eyes. Perch smiled. It wasn't meeting her parents, but it wasn't a bad second best.

Charlie came downstairs an hour later with his suitcase packed. He had explained to Perch that he really needed to get away. Although life was getting back on track after his latest operation

– he was playing sports again, the book was selling well and his family were wonderful – the recent theft of his Harley Davidson had got him a bit down about London life. And the chilly autumn in the city just made things worse.

'Don't I need to pack a bag too?' asked Perch.

'No,' replied Charlie with a grin. 'I've got everything we need.' Perch was disappointed as she liked the thought of taking her own suitcase.

'I've got another small surprise,' continued Charlie, choosing his words carefully to avoid any misunderstanding.

'What is it?'

Charlie glanced towards the window, and Perch followed his stare. Outside in the garden were Bells and Greystoke, waving their paws excitedly.

'That's nice of them to come and say goodbye,' said Perch, pleased to see her pals.

'They haven't come to say goodbye,' replied Charlie as he walked over and ushered the two cats into the house through the cat-flap in the garden door. 'They're coming with us.'

The three cats were all smiles, and playfully touched each other's paws. Greystoke was especially animated about the trip, armed with her knowledge from Professor Setting's amazing stories of far-off lands.

'It was too risky asking Snapper to come,' said Charlie. 'You could end up in all sorts of trouble with him around – he's a loose cannon. So, it's just the girl cats.'

Greystoke looked up, with a smarty-pants glint in her eye. 'Let's call it the Girls' Getaway,' she suggested.

'Yes, I like that,' Perch responded. 'The Girls' Getaway.' Bells nodded enthusiastically.

'But where exactly are we going?' Perch asked.

'I know,' interrupted Greystoke before Charlie could even answer. 'I bet we're going to the Catskills in America.' Charlie shook his head. Greystoke thought a bit more, and then tried again. 'Are we visiting the Catacombs in Paris?' Again Charlie shook his head. Greystoke summoned a last effort, but she just couldn't work it out. 'OK, we give up.'

Charlie waited a moment and then announced: 'We're going to North Africa, to Morocco.' He looked at Greystoke, whose smirk indicated that she now knew. Charlie waited so Greystoke could enjoy the moment.

'To the Catlas Mountains,' she told them all.

The airport was such amazing fun that it was almost like a holiday in itself. The cats skidded around on the vast shiny floor, while Charlie waited patiently in the queue for checking in. When he got to the front of the line he ordered the cats to lay low, as he didn't want the check-in girl behind the counter to notice.

'Just yourself off to Marrakech?' she asked with a welcoming smile. Perch wasn't surprised that she seemed to like Charlie – he was rather handsome.

'Just me,' replied Charlie without looking down. The cats grinned at each other, while Charlie loaded his one big suitcase onto the luggage belt.

'Any hand luggage?'

Charlie held up the two bags that he was going to take with him onto the aeroplane, one full and one rather empty. The empty bag was one of Charlie's large leather cricket bags, which usually held his pads, gloves and bats. The check-in girl nodded reassuringly, and told Charlie that the plane was leaving from Gate 16 in one hour, so he better go straight through customs and passport control.

First, however, Charlie needed to stop at the toilet. They all squeezed into one of the cubicles and Charlie locked the door.

'Now listen carefully,' said Charlie. 'We aren't allowed to take animals out of the country like this. If they catch us you'll all have to go into quarantine for a month.'

'What's quarantine?' asked Bells.

Charlie was about to answer but Greystoke jumped in. 'It means going into isolation, living by yourself in a small cell for a month, so they can check that you don't have any nasty diseases.' Bells shivered at the thought.

'That's right,' continued Charlie. 'Nobody wants that, so I'm going to put you all in this large bag and surround you with these cuddly toys, as well as a couple of cricket bats just in case we get searched.' Charlie rearranged the contents between the two bags and continued. 'With all the soft fur around, nobody will notice that you're real. I'll leave the zip a bit open so you can get some air.'

Greystoke looked doubtful, but it was Perch who spoke. 'What if we get hungry or thirsty?' she asked.

'That's why I've got these,' said Charlie, and he brought out of his pocket three envelopes full with tiny cat biscuits, shaped like little balls. He gave one envelope to each cat and showed them the bottle of water at the bottom of the bag. And then he put them all inside.

'You have to be still now,' Charlie said seriously. 'I can't speak to you at all until we're safely in Morocco.' And with that Charlie pulled up the zip, leaving it a little open, just as he had promised.

At first it was quite good fun inside the bag. The cats played hide-and-seek in between the soft toys, which was entertaining enough. Greystoke was brilliant at it and won most of the rounds, taking best advantage of the dark. At one point Perch, who was doing the searching, became annoyed because Greystoke was pretending not to be found. But then Perch realised that she hadn't been nudging Greystoke, but had been prodding a toy monkey instead.

After a while, however, the cats started to get bored. And hot too.

'Pass me the water,' pleaded a sweaty Perch, who was particularly irritable having hit her head on the handle of a cricket bat.

Greystoke looked concerned. 'Be sure to leave enough for all of us – it's 1352 miles to Morocco.'

'I'm hungry too,' said Perch, as she opened her envelope and stuck a couple more cat biscuits in her mouth. 'Gotta keep your energy up.'

Bells wasn't that hungry. She sat quietly at the back of the bag, thinking about all the things she liked about Snapper – his charm, his enthusiasm and zest for life, his playfulness, and how much he cared for her. The Girls' Getaway was great, but she missed her man. Bells took a biscuit out but accidentally tore the envelope. She placed the biscuit in her mouth, and tucked the remaining three behind her collar. You never know when you might need a snack, she thought.

Suddenly it went very dark in the bag. Greystoke's interest got the better of her and she popped her head out of the bag. Through the darkness she could just make out that Charlie had taken his jacket, shoes and belt off, and there were hoards of people queuing up behind him. She recognised that they were at the security check and Charlie was arguing with a customs officer about the bag in the X-ray machine. The bag that the cats were in.

'There's just a lot of soft toys in here,' stressed Charlie. 'For the Moroccan mountain children.'

'Now please stay calm, sir,' replied the customs officer. 'I thought I saw something move and I'm sure you understand that I have to check anything suspicious.' He pressed a button and the large cricket bag started to move towards him. Greystoke darted straight back inside and firmly whispered, 'STAY VERY STILL.'

The zip opened, light streamed in, and a large hand delved into the bag. The hand started rummaging around the soft toys, and grazed Perch's ear. Greystoke dodged the hand a couple of times, but then the hand seemed to settle on Bells' whiskers. The man's fingers were twiddling around and Perch could tell that Bells was trying desperately not to laugh. She was holding the chuckles in, desperately holding them in, but Bells shook her head as if to say she was going to have to let the laughter burst out. Perch sighed. It would be the end of the trip before it had really begun. But then the cats heard a shout from the crowd.

'Hey, that's Charlie Needle, England's cricket hero,' shouted a very excited man in the queue for the security check. Everyone looked over at Charlie, who blushed under his Hendon Hawks baseball cap.

'I thought I recognised you,' said the customs officer directly to Perch's owner. 'That's why you've got a cricket bag. I'm so sorry to have detained you. Would you mind signing this card for my son?'

'It would be a pleasure,' said Charlie, who zipped the bag up tightly and took it off the machine belt. A few minutes later they were all on the go again, and the gentle sway of Charlie's walking made all the tired cats doze off. And the next thing they knew the bag was being opened in a hotel room in steamy Marrakech.

∴•

The Hotel Splendid was a grand Moroccan building, and a sign in the foyer boasted that some decades ago the British prime minister Winston Churchill had been a frequent visitor. The room that Charlie had reserved was easily large enough for them all, with a big double bed and a separate lounge area where the cats would sleep. The bathroom was enormous and the marble floor was even skiddier than the floor at the airport. But the best thing about the room was the view from the balcony, over the lush hotel gardens and onto the Djemaa El Fna, the famous central square in Marrakech.

After an early supper, Charlie led the cats through the garden, where they climbed some unusually-shaped fig trees, and towards the square. The cats' ears pricked up with anticipation well before they got there. The noise of drums, music and laughter began to fill the air, as did a strange smell. Perch's nose started twitching as she absorbed the strong scent of spices, incense, smoke and the warm late autumn evening air. But the vibrant noise and the sweet smells couldn't prepare the cats for what they saw as they stepped into the Djemaa El Fna.

The square was, quite literally, alive with activity. Wherever Perch looked something was going on. There were acrobats doing summersaults in brightly-coloured clothes. Jugglers were using balls, pots and even daggers, sometimes juggling four or five at a time. Greystoke saw a man bend his head backwards and slowly swallow a long sword.

'He's going to have a bit of a sore throat,' she suggested, somewhat dumbstruck.

Bells couldn't stop herself from interjecting. 'It may not be very sensible, but it is kind of exciting.' Even Greystoke couldn't disagree.

Perch saw a man light a flame on a long stick and put it very close to his mouth as he looked up at the sky. She wondered what was going to happen as he lowered his head and stared straight at her. He took a deep breath in and then blew out with all his might. A fireball rocketed out of his mouth straight towards a motionless Perch, but evaporated into the air just before it reached her. People nearby clapped and laughed and even a startled Perch couldn't help but be enthralled.

Charlie led them around the square, which was teeming with local people and tourists, young and old. There were food stalls everywhere selling hot and cold nibbles, and Charlie bought them each a delicious kebab. When Bells had finished hers she was about to try and copy the sword-swallower with her kebab-skewer, but

Charlie grabbed it out of her paws just in time.

After an hour or so the cats were getting tired. All the excitement was exhausting, and this was still their first day. They were on their way back to the hotel when Greystoke and Bells stopped together, entranced by the beautiful recorder music played by a man sitting cross-legged on the ground. They wandered over to him and Perch and Charlie followed. Next to the man was a tall straw basket with the lid off. Bells was about to look inside but Greystoke pulled her back.

'I wouldn't do that,' she cautiously advised. 'Better to stand back and watch.'

So they did and out of the basket, to the sound of an eerie pipe tune, a white snake emerged and slowly uncoiled up into the air. Higher and higher rose the cobra, with its hooded head and a venomous tongue slipping in and out of its mouth. Perch was captivated and took a step closer to have better look. In a flash the snake snapped at her, darting forwards and spitting. Perch jumped back.

'So sorry,' said the snake charmer in a foreign accent. 'Snake no like animals.' He looked up at Charlie. 'American?'

Charlie shook his head and grabbed the cats in his strong arms. It had been a long day and he realised that they were getting exhausted.

'But I wanted to buy something,' said an irritable Bells.

'All in good time,' answered Charlie. And before long they were all back in the hotel and fast asleep.

The next few days flew by. They visited a wonderful fort where the cats climbed all over the canons, a lake palace where the king used to live and the Moroccan national museum – which everyone found boring except Greystoke. And every evening they went back into the Djemaa El Fna for their daily dose of exotic mystery and a chicken kebab.

The one exception was the day that Charlie took them on a bus to the city of Fez, which had the most famous souk in the world. The souk was like a market, but it took place in a dense area of tiny streets and lanes, covered by a canopy of material to keep the sun out. Throughout the lanes were stalls and shops selling all kinds of things – clothes like T-shirts and thin cotton trousers, jewellery, wallets and handbags, pointy slippers in a million different colours, and lots of small red hats that sat on your head like an upside down cup.

'I've seen a man on TV wear a hat like,' said Perch. 'All his

74

magic tricks went wrong, but he was very funny.'

'Yes, I've seen him too,' said Bells. 'He was funny, but sad too. And he never looked very well.'

Perch and Bells were by themselves in the souk because Greystoke had decided to watch the chess game being played at a café outside the market entrance, and Charlie had gone off to look for a present for Anna. They had all agreed to meet at the café after one hour.

As the two cats walked together down the busy lane, Perch looked over her shoulder and had a real loving moment. Bells was beautiful and had become such an adorable and uncomplicated friend. In her cheerful manner she accepted Perch as she was and was always supportive if Perch was ever upset.

'I'd like you to try this on,' said Perch, who had picked out from a jewellery stall the most gorgeous necklace, with pieces of stunning rose quartz in between tiny slithers of bronze. Bells obliged and the necklace hung prettily beneath her collar – she looked gorgeous and when she moved her head the necklace made a delicate tinkling sound, just like wind chimes.

'But you can't afford this,' she stated to Perch.

'Don't you worry about that,' answered Perch, whose sixth sense seemed to be guiding her. Before Bells knew it, Perch had bargained a price with the storekeeper and the treasure belonged to Bells. When they met the others a few minutes later the compliments flowed, but Charlie seemed to have other things on his mind.

'Come on,' he said. 'We better get back as you all need your

energy for tomorrow.' And then the cats remembered.
Tomorrow was the highlight of the whole trip, climbing to the
top of Mount Toubkal.

The taxi first took the cats to the small village of Imlil, nestled at
the bottom of the Catlas mountains. The one-hour journey
from Marrakech had upset everyone's stomachs, twisting and
turning along the mountain roads, and they all looked a bit green
as they trudged over to the village store.

'We won't need much,' said Charlie. 'I've checked in the
guidebook and the guesthouse at the base camp has all the food
we need. I'll just make sure we have enough water.'

As the cats lolled around in the sunshine, Charlie went off
to look for what he called the most important thing. Fifteen
minutes later he was back, but not alone.

'I'd like you to meet Mohammed,' announced Charlie as he
introduced a young, handsome Moroccan man, about eighteen
years old, with a friendly, warm face and dressed in a traditional
cloak.

Mohammed bowed gently. 'Salaam aleikum.' The cats
looked at each other, giggled and bowed back. Mohammed
smiled.

'And I'd also like you to meet Jasmine and Percy,' continued
Charlie. Perch looked over and behind Charlie were two dark
brown donkeys, saddled up and ready to go.

'But where am I going to sit?' asked Bells. Greystoke was
similarly concerned as dividing two by five just didn't work.

'Well, I'm going to ride on Percy,' Charlie responded. 'And
you three will ride Jasmine. And our guide Mohammed will

walk ahead and lead us all up into the mountains.'

'Must go now,' prompted Mohammed. 'Only four hours before he is night.'

'It is night. Before *it* is night,' corrected Greystoke.

'Yes,' repeated Mohammed. 'Before he is night.'

Greystoke was about to say something but Perch interrupted. 'Oh, leave the poor boy alone,' she said. 'After all, how much Arabic do you know, Greystoke?' Fair enough, thought the clever clogs cat. And, with no time to lose, they were off.

The Catlas Mountains were rather beautiful, but not in the usual way. They were nothing like the rolling green peaks of the Lake District, and certainly didn't resemble the grassy Alps, and they weren't as striking as the Himalayas. No, the Catlas Mountains were really quite dry, barren and rocky, but this made them quite special – they looked like mountains at the beginning of time.

'Look,' shouted Perch as she noticed a rare handful of wild flowers, these ones yellow, protruding from the soil behind a large boulder. They all looked immediately but were most surprised, not by the flowers, but by Perch's voice, which echoed around the mountains, as if she was repeating herself.

Bells couldn't wait to have a go. 'Hello!' she screamed as loud as she could. 'Hello ... Hello ... Helloww ... Hellooww,' came the ever quieter echoes.

Up and up they climbed, with the gentle wind getting progressively cooler as the sunlight slowly faded. Mohammed steered them along the mountain paths, checking regularly that they were all OK, and feeding the donkeys the occasional carrot. Just before it was dark Charlie noticed a single house in the distance, and Mohammed grinned to indicate that they had reached their destination.

The wooden lodge was the base that climbers used before making an ascent to the top of Mount Toubkal, the highest peak in the Catlas Mountains. Climbers would rest for the night, then start the steep climb to the top at sunrise, which was at about five in the morning at this time of year. It normally took around four hours to get to the top and two to get back down, meaning one was back in the lodge before the dreadful heat of the midday sun.

Charlie had a chat with the owner and paid for a very basic room with bunk beds – Charlie would sleep on the bottom and the cats on top. Perch and Bells were having a great time racing up and down the bunk-bed ladder when Charlie returned to the room, looking downcast.

'I'm afraid there's no food,' he explained.

'But you checked the guidebook,' replied Greystoke. 'And I did too. It clearly said that food and water could be bought at the base camp lodge.'

'I guess you just can't trust the guidebook,' said Charlie solemnly. 'This is all I've got.' He took out of his pocket four triangles of Dairylea cheese, and held them out on his hand. 'Better save them for breakfast,' Charlie suggested.

'But I'm starving,' said Bells. There was little they could do, though, as the owner had nothing to sell and had only enough water for Charlie to fill up one small bottle. Yet there was worse to come, when a group of German tourists took hunks of bread and cheese out of their backpacks and started cooking sausages on the grill. The delicious smell filled the lodge and Charlie and the cats looked on jealously. But the Germans just carried on, drinking beer and laughing loudly.

'Alvays be prepared,' shouted a man with a moustache in Perch's direction, as he guzzled another Bratwurst.

'Come on,' said Charlie sadly as they all sloped off. 'Let's get some rest – we've got an early start.'

As we know, Perch had never really been a morning cat, and the next day was no exception. It was hard to even call it morning because at four-thirty it was still dark outside; but, by the time they had all got their belongings together and stepped outside, a hazy light was beginning to appear on the horizon.

'Pretty beautiful, eh?' asked Charlie as he stared at the silhouetted mountains. The cats nodded. 'Glad you came?' Charlie continued. And, once again, a synchronous nod.

'We better have these now,' said Charlie as he handed out one cheese triangle to each of them. 'Chew it well, and make it last.'

The initial climbing was fine and even good fun. First there was a scree slope covered in gravel, where the cats seemed to walk two steps upward just to slide one step back down again. Next, a winding track weaved between rocks, steadily leading them higher and higher. Charlie was sure-footed and was always in front, showing the way. He said he was like a mountain goat but he didn't look like one.

The problem, however, was the sun. By seven o'clock they had been going for two hours and the sun had risen in the clear blue sky, making it already very hot. The group stopped for some water, but they hadn't been able to get any more at the lodge, meaning they only had Charlie's one flask to share. And they were already parched.

'I could drink a reservoir,' joked Bells.

'I don't think you actually could,' replied Greystoke. 'There's at least 300,000 litres of water in a small reservoir.' Perch listened on, knowing the cats were hungry, thirsty and grumpy, while at the same time trying to get the thought of the lovely cool pond in Charlie's garden out of her mind.

'Not far to go,' chipped in Charlie. 'We can do it.' He was both perky and determined. After all, you don't get to be England cricket captain without a fair bit of guts and determination.

So they set off again, but it was tough. Sometimes tracks met other tracks but there were no signposts. Charlie suggested that so long as they kept going up they would get there in the end. But every time it looked as if they had reached the top, another peak appeared further ahead. Charlie was pressing on, but the cats were becoming exhausted, and the distance between them was increasing. Perch reckoned that she was about fifty metres behind Charlie, Greystoke was another twenty metres behind Perch, and Bells was a further one hundred metres behind. Perch had been glancing back regularly to check, but eventually she stopped in the shade of a large rock for a break to be joined a couple of minutes later by Greystoke. They chatted and waited for Bells to join them, but she didn't. Perch glanced down the hill.

'Where's Bells gone?' she asked. But Greystoke had no idea, so they retraced their steps. They looked round every nook and cranny but there was no sign of their dear friend. The noisy howling wind didn't help either, as they shouted out Bells' name over and over. The wind also meant Charlie couldn't hear them, though luckily he had wondered what had happened and had returned down the hill to find the anxious duo.

For an hour, the three of them – Charlie, Perch and Greystoke – searched around the area, screaming Bells' name, but to no effect. They had lost her. Mindful of the baking midday sun, Charlie called them together.

'We have to go back,' he stated sadly.

'But we can't leave Bells … we can't …' pleaded a desperate Perch. 'She's my best friend, and she'll die out here.'

'We'll all die out here,' responded Charlie, 'if we don't get back and get some more water.'

Perch looked to Greystoke for support, but the sensible cat was looking glumly down at the ground, knowing that what Charlie said was true. They could all perish if they didn't get back soon.

'I won't go!' said Perch. 'I won't leave her alone on a mountain.' But Charlie knew that he had to take control, so he picked Perch and Greystoke up and started the walk back down.

'No … no … no …' begged a sobbing Perch, but even she was beginning to realise that there was no choice.

Eventually, the cats fell asleep in Charlie's arms and weren't even aware that it took Charlie another three hours to get back down. At the lodge, the cats woke up briefly as the sun was setting. Charlie had managed to get a small bottle of water from the German tourists, which they all shared. Mohammed had been able to get a little bread from a fellow guide, but nobody was very hungry. They all went to bed early and at first light began the descent back to Imlil.

Bells hadn't died though. What had happened was this. As they had all been climbing the mountain, Bells had gradually got further behind the others, until she couldn't even see Perch up ahead of her. At one point she had to choose between two tracks and, unluckily, she picked the wrong one. The track wound around the mountainside until it ended in a narrow ledge. On all sides of the ledge was a sheer drop, and it was too dangerous to turn around. Bells yelled repeatedly for help, but the wind was loud and strong and there was no chance of anybody hearing her. She became desperate and exhausted, and eventually collapsed into unconsciousness on the ledge.

Bells was lucky though. Two young shepherd boys had been out on the mountain and had found her on the ledge. They knew Bells was alive because she was still warm, so they picked her up and took her to their village of mud and rock houses carved out of the mountainside. When Bells woke, she was astonished to find herself in a cool room with a stone floor and a saucer of water next to her. She helped herself to a drink, but noticed that it was dark outside and soon drifted off once again into a deep sleep.

When Bells next woke up it was clearly early morning, and the boys were trying to get her to play with them. She was grateful and didn't want to appear rude, but she had no energy. So she just smiled and licked them in appreciation for saving her life. She looked around at the tiny passages between the huts and houses, everything muddied and dirty. This was a true mountain village, charming and traditional, but no place for a city cat to live out her years. She was desperate and gazed out of the window with a forlorn expression.

Meanwhile, Charlie and the others had begun their descent that morning. Everyone was miserable, even Mohammed, but they had no choice – and still no food. The donkeys, Percy and Jasmine, seemed the only ones to be content as they carried Charlie, Perch and Greystoke back down towards Imlil.

Without anything to eat, Perch was very light-headed. Maybe it was mountain sickness, but as she stared from the top of the donkey everything around her seemed to be going backwards and forwards. She complained to the others but everyone seemed to feel the same.

'Look over there,' Perch suddenly said, pointing at a distant mountainside.

'What is it?' asked Greystoke, squinting. 'I can't see anything.'

'There are houses that look like they've been cut out of the mountain.'

Greystoke strained her eyes. 'I think you're imagining things, it's just the haze.'

But Charlie corrected her. 'No, Perch is right. It's a mountain village.'

It was at that very moment that Bells, staring out of the window, saw the donkeys in the distance, with what she thought were people and cats atop. She couldn't believe it. But those donkeys were walking down the mountain path pretty fast and would soon be past the village. She only had one chance and tried to meow as loud as she could. But she had no strength and her throat was terribly raw and dry. Not a sound came out. She watched, almost paralysed, as her opportunity seemed to be disappearing. If she didn't get their attention now she would be in the village forever.

Bells' head sunk low in sadness and her chin touched something. It was the necklace that Perch had bought her that tinkled like wind chimes. She may have been unable to meow but she could shake her head. Bells mustered what strength she had, and a gentle sound came from her neck and carried on the wind.

Perch's ears pricked up.

'What's that?' she shouted to the others.

'What's what?' asked Charlie.

'That noise.' They all listened but could hear nothing. So the donkeys started off again.

Bells watched, but realised that they were carrying on. She had to be able to make a louder sound but had no strength whatsoever, and there was no food in the room to give her strength. A tear appeared in the corner of her eye and rolled down her cheek and onto her neck, ending up on her collar. She lifted a paw to wipe the tear off and felt something underneath the collar. What was it? She picked out something semi-hard that appeared edible. Then she remembered … the biscuits she had tucked under her collar. She reached down, found two more, and shoved them into her mouth. Within a few moments she was feeling a little stronger, and she shook her head as if her life depended on it. Which it did.

Even Mohammed stopped this time, and he brought the donkeys to a halt.

'I can hear it now too,' said Charlie. 'It's a message from the village. Someone's trying to tell us something.'

Perch dived off the donkey and charged towards the village, finding strength from nowhere to dive over rocks and boulders. When she got close to the houses she stopped briefly, then sprang again and jumped straight through a window and into her dear friend's arms.

'My darling, you're OK,' said a delighted Perch. Bells nodded and pointed to her throat to indicate that she couldn't speak. But her tears said it all, along with the warmth of her embrace.

The others soon joined Perch and Bells, and they were filled with relief and happiness. Mohammed explained to the two shepherd boys what had happened and, before they knew it, all the other villagers had joined them.

Charlie noticed a number of the children had infected mosquito bites on their bodies, so he took out his travel medicines and put antibiotic cream and plasters on them. Then Charlie played cricket with all of the children, and when he got tired he gave them his bats and balls to keep. He also gave an elderly man, the leader of the village, all of the medicines to help cure the infections.

The cats, however, just sat contentedly on the stone floor. Nothing could beat the feeling of all being together again. The boys had brought them a bowl of goat's milk each. It might not have been a coffee shop frothy special, but it tasted like heaven. And when they arrived home in Crouch End the following day, after a perfect night's sleep in the hotel, they had the best story ever to tell.

And Perch was never quite sure if it had all been a dream or not …

Chapter 6

Behind Bars (Again)

It was a beautifully sunny, but very cold, morning in early January when Perch awoke sharply. The crisp winter air meant that her brain was already in full flow, and the idea that she had been developing all week seemed suddenly clear. Ever since the adventure with Crazybones, Perch had felt that she needed to know more about the sad cat's life. And what fascinated Perch most was Crazybones' last few days in prison – when the innocent cat knew that he was going to perish.

Perch bounded out of her basket and headed for the phone. She was going to ask Snapper to come with her again, but then imagined that Bells might not be too pleased, so decided that this was something she needed to do alone. Charlie was up in Lancashire with his family – so he wouldn't notice that Perch was gone – and by half past seven, before she had even licked herself all over or taken her morning milk, Perch was out the house and walking down Cecile Park.

As Perch approached the bus stop, something rather important dawned upon her. Perch knew that Crazybones had been kept in Alcatraz, a prison on the Isle of Dogs, surrounded on all sides by the river Thames. But, like most cats, Perch did not like water, and she knew that she would definitely not be able to stomach the ferry ride to the island prison. There was clearly only one thing for it so Perch headed up Crouch Hill, straight for the Old Curiosity Shop.

Despite its rather English name, the Old Curiosity Shop was owned by a Chinese man, called Fu Kung. As Perch entered she felt like she was going back in time. The air was full of dust and incense, cobwebs lurked in the ceiling corners, and old ornaments adorned every nook and cranny of the cluttered shop. Fu Kung was nowhere to be seen, which was good news as he didn't like animals at all. It was Alfred who had told Perch about the shop and how once Fu Kung had kicked Alfred out on his bottom, just because he didn't like the smell of dogs.

It was also Alfred who had informed Perch of the shop's magical powers, which was precisely why Perch was there. According to Alfred, on the highest shelf – just behind the Ming vases – was a magic lantern which, if rubbed, would transport you directly to any place you wanted to be. With this goal in mind, Perch tiptoed in as quietly as she could, only to be thwarted by the shop bell tinkling as the door opened.

'Who go there? I no see you. Come where I see you,' sounded an old Chinese man's voice out of the mist from the far side of the shop.

Perch knew she didn't have long and looked around eagerly. She saw cups, glasses, wooden furniture and old kettles and pans. But not what she was looking for. So she spun around to look elsewhere and, as she turned, her paw knocked a large porcelain pot from its stand. It wobbled and wobbled, but with lightning cat reactions Perch used her other front paw and her forehead to stop it crashing to the ground.

Phew, she thought to herself. That looks expensive.

'I hear you, now I see you,' shouted a closer voice. 'Leave precious Ming vase alone you clumsy cat! I kick you out on your bottom.'

The *vases*, Perch twigged, and glanced directly behind them. In a row stood three old-fashioned Chinese lanterns. One was very ornate and looked like it was made of gold, the second was bronze with jewels inlaid and the third was just a simple brass lantern, nothing fussy and no precious stones. Perch knew her bible stories and had watched lots of Indiana Jones films, so she grabbed the simple one. As Fu Kung's slender hands, with long nails on the fifth fingers, reached out, Perch rubbed the lantern vigorously against her fur. She closed her eyes, firmly said the words 'Alcatraz, Alcatraz' and, in a flash of smoke, she was gone.

As well as the many people who have resided in Alcatraz over the years, there have also been a number of notorious household pets. They too have had to pay their debt to society, and have done so in the Domestic Crimanimal Wing (DCA). With their sometimes unpredictable personalities, such prisoners have mostly been cats, but the occasional dog and one or two pet rats have also had to serve their time. It was outside the gates of this huge, scary building that Perch suddenly found herself, on her special visit to see the very cell where Crazybones spent his last remaining days on this earth.

As Perch looked up she felt a shiver of nerves and excitement. There were guards positioned all around the high walls and gates, and even more standing inside the tall tower that overlooked the main yard. She shuffled into the line of visitors and waited behind the others who were signing in.

'Are you seeing an in*cat*, or just here for the tour?' asked the smiley lady at the front desk, as Perch stamped her paw in the visitors' book. Perch pointed politely at the poster behind the woman's head that advertised the prison tour.

'Well, in that case,' continued the chirpy woman, 'you'll be wanting Mr Sentry to show you around with the tour group. After all, we wouldn't want you wandering off by yourself and getting banged up with a bunch of hardened crim*animals* now would we?'

The woman let out a throaty laugh and licked her fat lips. Perch nodded anxiously, forcing a little smile of her own while getting somewhat hot under the collar. Just then, she felt a firm hand on her shoulder. It was Mr Sentry, the head prison guard. He grabbed the lantern, as visitors were clearly not allowed to bring anything into the prison, and promised it would be returned at the end. There was no turning back now.

The tour started in the basement where they kept all the cells. As Perch made her way through the long corridor she spotted mostly cats, a few dogs, two rats and a particularly nasty-looking parrot. Although some of them looked a bit mean, most of them just seemed sad to her. It's not much of a life for an animal, thought Perch, even a domestic one, being stuck in a cell with only a litter tray and a scratchy woollen blanket for company.

As the tour group was escorted further down the main corridor, Perch's thoughts were interrupted by a deep voice.

'Hey there pretty lady, you look lonely. Why don't you scootch up closer and Big Daddy will put a smile on your face.'

'No cat-calling!' snapped Mr Sentry, as he rapped a fistful of keys against the bars of a large tabby's cell. 'I don't want to tell you again, Big Daddy.'

'Sorry, boss,' came the sarcastic reply. 'I'm only animal after all.' He slumped back into the darkness of his tiny room. A moment later, Mr Sentry stopped and opened the doors of a nearby cell.

'Here we are, Miss. This is it – the space that I believe you wished to see. I'll be back after my rounds to pick you up.' And he was off with the rest of the group, leaving Perch all alone, facing the very place, the small, dark, slightly pongy cell, that once belonged to Crazybones himself.

Perch looked around. She saw the small bed with the scratchy woollen blanket, an old writing table and above it a tiny window too high to see through. The window was locked from the outside and had bars on the inside, meaning escape was impossible. The sight of the bars sent a shiver down Perch's spine, as memories of the pet-shop cage flooded back. She sat down on the bed and shed a tear as she imagined what it must have been like for poor old Crazybones, alone in the cell, with the thoughts of being hanged by the scruff of his neck keeping him awake at night. As her eyes dropped downward she saw, etched into the dark wood of the desk, the last written words of that famous cat. They read:

"Believe me, I am innocent – C.Bones."

Perch had seen enough and was more than ready to return to Crouch End, back to her home comforts and to those who loved her best. She headed out of the

cell without looking back and made her way down the corridor through which she had come, towards the group returning with Mr Sentry. Just then a loud bell rang and, one by one, the doors of each cell opened to allow the animals into the yard for exercise time. Perch quickened her pace, not wanting to get too close to some of the rougher-looking characters, and reached Mr Sentry just as he announced a warning.

'Stay close everyone. You're fine with me, but don't go straying off now.' There was a slight chuckle to Mr Sentry's advice, as if he enjoyed the tour group's nervousness.

Now, all this time, Perch had not been aware that she was being carefully watched. In fact, from the very moment she had gone down to the cells she had unknowingly become in mortal danger. Sitting opposite her in the corridor, hidden in the shadows, was a very sly, clever cat called GingerMac. He had acquired this name for two reasons. First, and obviously, he was ginger. And second, this nasty character had a taste for using knives, and had been imprisoned for randomly cutting up clothes and newspapers in shops. His nickname in the cat criminal world was Mac the Knife.

As soon as GingerMac had set eyes on Perch, he had sensed that she was the answer to his prayers for a tenth life. When he spotted the colour of her coat, and her sea-blue eyes the shape of almonds, the effeminate cat knew precisely what to do. The similarity between them was undeniable. They could easily be mistaken for brother

and sister or, as he cunningly realised, for each other.

GingerMac hatched his devilish plan, to swap places with the curious visitor and to escape prison once and for all.

Perch, of course, knew nothing of this, and was just pleased to be back with the others.

'I'm sorry it took us so long to get back to you,' apologised Mr Sentry. 'But there's been a catfight down in Cell Block H. We'll need to wait here for a few minutes until it's all settled down.'

'In that case,' said Perch, 'could you please direct me to the toilet. I've been bursting since I arrived.' Mr Sentry pointed towards a nearby green door and said that they would all wait until Perch returned.

Perch was whistling quietly to herself as she entered the toilet and was pleasantly surprised at how clean it was. She chose the second cubicle along and shut the door before sitting down on the loo. Perch was so relieved at being able to finally pee that she paid little attention to the strange scraping sound outside her cubicle door. When she had finished she pushed the door to get out. But she couldn't open it. Harder and harder she pressed, but the door wouldn't budge. Perch thought she heard a sneaky laugh, and then soft paw steps making their way towards the main toilet door. Perch wasn't one to panic, but this clearly wasn't good.

What had happened was this. The scheming GingerMac was rather observant and had noticed from Perch's pained expression earlier that it was only partly due to emotion that she had sat cross-pawed on the bed for so long in Crazybones' cell. The other reason was obviously that she needed the loo, and GingerMac had been waiting patiently, and secretively, to put his toilet identity swap plan into action. He had slipped through the green door straight after Perch and, as soon as she was in the cubicle, had pushed a cupboard over to stop her getting out.

If Mr Sentry had been a cat, or indeed a hamster for that matter, he might have easily spotted the difference between the two pusses. But being just an ordinary man – and a dreadfully busy one at that – Mr Sentry didn't suspect for a moment that the cat coming out of the green door was a convicted feline, while an innocent Perch banged her paws helplessly against the doors.

'Goodbye, young lady, mind how you go,' cried Mr Sentry a few minutes later, as he locked the main prison gates behind the last of the departing tour group. He didn't recall the ginger cat looking so evidently smug when it had arrived.

'Goodbye, sucker,' smirked GingerMac as he picked up his pace outside the prison, until all that could be seen of him was a dark spot on the horizon, jumping and whooping for joy.

After some time, and quite a lot of effort, Perch finally managed to squeeze under the cubicle door, wishing she hadn't drunk so much full cream milk at Charlie's house. As she emerged from the toilet, though, Perch was surprised not to find Mr Sentry waiting for her. She made her way nervously across the corridor, only to be stopped in her tracks by a booming voice.

'And where do you think you're going, sonny?' The voice was attached to a red-headed, red-faced guard with seriously bad breath.

'I think I'm ready to go home now if you please,' replied Perch politely.

'I'm sure you are, mate – you and the rest of them,' bellowed the response, ending in a loud laugh. 'Now back to your cell, GingerMac, before I call the boss.'

And before Perch could say "Ginger who?" she was being not-so-gently frog-marched back to the cells. She tried not to look towards the guard, who she was sure had just eaten a cheese and pickled onion sandwich.

'We'll take him down guv'nor,' came the voice from one of two scrawny, mean-looking black cats. 'Heading that way anyway … save you the bovver.'

'Thanks, Brutus,' replied the guard. 'Kind of you – I'll go and get something to eat.' And with that, the guard left Perch alone in the company of two unsavoury characters, each as dark and scraggly as the other.

'Okay, Macco, where's our winnings?' asked the one that the guard had called Brutus, pressing his bony paw into Perch's ribs. Perch looked at the two of them blankly. 'What, cat got your tongue?' continued the villain. 'Our winnings from last night, GingerMac, those five tins of rabbit-flavour Whiskers that you lost at poker.'

Perch stared at them dumbly, before she finally plucked up the courage to reply. 'Mac who? What cat-food are you talking about? I don't even like rabbit flavour.'

The darker one of the two, who Perch later found out was called Nero, grabbed her by the scruff of the neck and grizzled in her ear. 'You better have it by midnight tomorrow, sunshine, or you'll wish you never set foot in this place.' Too late, I wish that already, thought Perch, as she was shoved inside GingerMac's cell.

After a dreadful night's sleep, uncomfortable on the scratchy blanket in the claustrophobic space, Perch awoke to the sound of clinking iron as the cell doors opened. Perch had given up trying to convince anybody of the mistake, and had accepted that she was just another *scat*istic. This morning would provide her introduction to the daily routine in the CDA wing of Alcatraz.

After a horrid breakfast, with no milk or kippers, Perch was herded around the building with the other incats, until she reached a room with a guard seated at a desk.

'Carpentry or library today, GingerMac?' asked the guard, who was checking people in for their morning duty.

'Library,' suggested Perch by pointing at a book behind the guard, opting for the work that she hoped would put her in contact with a better class of pet. And besides, she didn't fancy the idea of some of these crimanimals with a hammer in their paws. As Perch made her way through the library doors, however, her mind was restless with thoughts of how on earth she might come by five tins of cat food by midnight.

In the library, Perch was first tasked with putting books that had been borrowed and returned back on the shelves. The work was undemanding but gradually took Perch's mind off things, and she even began to enjoy the challenge of making sure each book went back into exactly the correct place. She could easily reach the lower shelves, but Perch was high up on the ladder when the accident happened.

Two books had been labelled as needing replacing in the unpopular Autobiography section, which was on the top shelf. Perch popped the first book, all about David Beckham, into its place, and looked down at the next.

The gasp that came from Perch, and the thump a few moments later as she hit the ground, was heard by all in the library. Cats ran over to find out if their fellow was alright, only to find an unconscious ginger cat on the floor with a book sprawled next to her. The cover was clear: *A Right Charlie: My Life Up To Now.*

Perch remembered none of this of course, and found herself waking up, about a minute later, as if from a deep, deep sleep. Through the haze she saw cat heads staring down at her and was comforted by a sensitive, velvety voice, repeating the same thing over and over.

'Don't worry, son, you're alright ... just open your eyes to the world.'

It turned out that the gentle soul who helped Perch up from her fall was named Morgan, but everyone called him Old Velvet on account of his velvety voice and his advanced age. In human years he was about eighty. Old Velvet's fur was a matt black colour, greying and slightly straggly at the ends and, in spite of his age, he was still a handsome specimen.

Over the next few days, Old Velvet and Perch were to become the best of friends, but in those first few hours he took her under his wing. First they just sat quietly in the corner while Perch recovered, letting the silence speak. Then, as Perch gradually
perked up, he listened intently as she related her life story,

ending with her mistaken identity prison experience. At the end he looked her sympathetically in the eye.

'We all have our stories, honey,' he said. 'But best not to dwell, and just get on with things.'

If anybody else had said such words they would have sounded dismissive, but Old Velvet clearly believed and understood Perch, though knew that there was little that anyone could do about it.

'And what about you?' asked Perch. 'What's your story. How did you get here?'

'It's been so long,' replied the old-timer, 'that I can hardly remember.'

'Oh come on,' urged Perch. 'I know you can.' Old Velvet sighed and slowly recounted his tale.

'I was a young lad when I came in here. Not a kitten, but not a grown cat either. In between. I had been abandoned by my owners and was walking the back streets behind Camden Market. I hadn't eaten for days and was starving, but it was a very hot day and my throat was parched. The back door to a flat by the canal was open, and on the kitchen table was a full bottle of milk, with water dripping down the outside as if straight out of the fridge. I knew it was wrong, but I couldn't help myself.'

'You took the milk,' came in Perch eagerly.

'I tried to, but never got a lick. I knocked the bottle over and the owner ran in. My luck, he was a policeman, and the next thing I knew I'd been sentenced to life in this prison.'

'But that's not fair,' said Perch angrily.

'Life's not always fair,' was the reply. 'But that's my story.'

During the afternoon, Perch found she was pretty suited to library duty. She liked the others there – Jake, Flossy and particularly Madsy, a long-haired cat with curly whiskers and a clever word to say on any subject. She enjoyed sorting the books by size and subject, and soon realised that she had a real talent for reading aloud to those who, for whatever reason, couldn't read themselves. Perch's timing and expressiveness were spot-on, and her scarier voices made some of the younger cats' hair stand on end. After one story all the listeners clapped loudly, and Perch enjoyed her round of acclaws.

By teatime Perch's audience had grown in numbers, and by dinnertime she had collected one ball of string, three sardines and five cartons of Whiskers

in payment for her valuable services. Problem sorted, she thought. Well … almost. All she now had to do was find a way out of one of the best guarded facilities known to domestic animalkind.

∴•∴

'So, where's our winnings, Macco?' asked Brutus aggressively in the exercise yard in the early evening of the same day. He had Perch pinned against the yard wall.

'You said I had 'til midnight tonight,' replied Perch nervously. 'And, by the way, I told you before that my name's not Macco, it's P…'

'I don't care what your name is!' interrupted Brutus loudly. 'And, I changed my mind, I want my winnings now.' Perch glanced over at Old Velvet, who was being held with his paw behind his back by Brutus' unpleasant side-cat, Nero. Perch thought that poor Old Velvet was a bit long in the whisker for this kind of nonsense, and she was worried about his heart holding out. The guards were clearly not going to help, as they had all turned their backs on the disturbance.

'I've got it anyway,' she said defensively, and handed over the five precious tins of rabbit-flavour cat food. Brutus was clearly surprised.

'Oh … good … thanks. And … well done, I suppose.' No cat had ever delivered on time before, and he was obviously impressed.

Noticing the commotion, Big Daddy ambled over from the centre of the yard. He didn't like being far away from the centre of the action.

'What's going on 'ere then?' he asked.

'Macco paid up on time', responded Nero, as he released a ruffled Old Velvet from his grasp.

'Good on ya,' said Big Daddy in a jolly voice. 'These two are alright,' he continued, pointing at Perch and Old Velvet. 'They pay their dues, and I hear Macco's been spinning some fine yarns in the library. We'll make sure they stay safe – won't we, boys?' Brutus and Nero nodded, and Perch was getting a better idea of the incat hierarchy.

The following days went by in something of a haze of similarity for Perch. Each morning she awoke in Macco's cell, to the sound of a truncheon being rapped against the cell bars. An early stretch would help with the backache from the hard bed, before a tasteless breakfast in the canteen. Then it was library duty, where she split her time between her chores, being engrossed in conversation with Old Velvet, and telling stories to her growing band of avid listeners. Then the exercise yard, dinner and bed.

By the end of the first week in prison two significant things had happened. First, Perch's friendship with Old Velvet had blossomed, with the two cats enthralled by each other's company. Perch was struck by her older companion's take on life, a mixture of sadness and understated wisdom of the cat condition. And Old Velvet was enraptured by Perch's sympathetic personality and her loving loyalty. They weren't cell-mates, but they were becoming soulmates.

The second thing that happened was that Perch was developing into quite a star in the prison. Not only was she widely liked, but her storytelling was becoming legendary. And with such acceptance came benefits. Protection through Big Daddy and his lackeys meant Perch wasn't troubled by some of the other, unpleasant incats. And she also became privileged in terms of information, especially in relation to escape.

She knew, for example, that the Italian cat Angelo was using a stolen sculpting hammer to dig through his cell wall in Block M. Perch was also taken to see the top-secret glider being built in the H-Block attic by an ex-military cat whose nickname was "The Colonel" (though his real name was Biggles). Perch doubted the rickety glider would actually fly.

Perch's privileged position meant she was even included in one particular escape plan, when approached by Brutus one afternoon in the yard.

'There's a football match tomorrow, Macco,' he whispered furtively. 'Guards against incats. While the game's going on, a few of us are going to nip over the wall, using the ladder we made in carpentry. The lads are gonna let the guards win the match so they'll be distracted, but the victory will really be ours.' Brutus grinned slyly and continued. 'You're welcome to join us.'

Perch was about to decline the kind offer, as she was worried that if she was caught her sentence would be lengthened. But then Perch's thoughts wandered back to Charlie, and to her great buddies – Bells, Greystoke, Snapper and Alfred. As much as she enjoyed spending time with Old Velvet, she missed her pals sorely.

'I'm in!' she responded, and Brutus' whiskers fanned out as he grinned cheekily.

Perch spent that night tossing and turning in her cold bed. Had she made the right decision? If she was caught she might have to spend the rest of her life in the stinky cell, an appalling prospect. Perch wasn't a risk-taker like Snapper, and normally she would have avoided something as dangerous as a jailbreak. But these were not normal times: they were desperate times, and desperate times called for desperate measures.

When the next day dawned, Perch had hardly slept a wink. She was weary but strangely alert. The morning passed by as normal, and by three in the afternoon almost the whole prison was out in the yard for the long-awaited football match. The guards wore blue and the cats were in shirts with black hoops. Perch was a substitute, sitting on a bench close to the lowest part of the prison wall. Big Daddy and his henchmen were also on the bench. Perch was so nervous that she could feel her heart pounding inside her chest.

The game
started evenly,
with both sides
having a couple of
early chances, but
by half-time the
guards were one
goal up. The

feline team looked downcast during the break, but were geed up
by an inspirational pep-talk from Old Velvet – and by some
orange slices. Within three minutes of the restart, the cats scored
and the crowd went wild. This was clearly the cue and Perch
saw the ladder being secretively carried around the back of the
pitch; she was so worried that Perch wondered if she was going
to be sick. But it was too late now – there was no turning back.

Suddenly, as Perch sat there anxiously waiting for the escape

signal, a firm hand clasped her back.
Perch almost jumped out of her skin
when she turned around and saw Mr
Sentry, the head guard, standing behind
her.

'Come with me, Macco, now,' he said
rather assertively into Perch's ear. She imagined he must have
found out about the plan, and Perch looked helplessly at her
fellow escapees. But they certainly couldn't aid her, and Perch
trudged off with Mr Sentry back to her cell. As she sat on her
bed, Perch was about to tell Mr Sentry that the escape plot
hadn't been her idea, but she missed her chance as he jumped in
first.

'There's been a terrible mistake,' Mr Sentry began. Perch's
ears pricked up – she wondered if it was a trick.

'We know you're not Macco,' continued Mr Sentry. 'You see, we've found Macco. He was at St Pancras International station, trying to board a train to France. But old Macco couldn't help himself. He was in Marks and Spencer and liked the look of the cheese selection; he tried to steal it from the shop, and had his knives all ready to cut the cheese into bite-size pieces.'

'Those platters *are* very nice,' interrupted Perch, who then realised that her stomach wasn't the most important thing here. 'What happened to him?' she asked eagerly.

'A policeman got a tip-off,' Mr Sentry carried on. 'From a tall man with a dark coat and a wide-brimmed hat. The copper caught Macco red-handed and turned to thank the man, but apparently he had disappeared.' Something was jogged in Perch's memory at the mention of the stranger with the hat, but she couldn't quite make the connection.

'The policeman brought the felon here,' continued Mr Sentry, 'where Macco owned up to everything – including tricking you in the toilet. The warden's asked me to give you an unreserved apology on behalf of the prison.'

Fat lot of good that is, thought Perch, having lost several days of her life to the stupid identity error. She pondered carefully.

'If there's anything we can do to make up for this dreadful …'

'There is something you can do for me,' Perch jumped in. 'Old Velvet is, well, very old, and I want him released immediately.'

'Can't be done,' responded Mr Sentry. 'He's a lifer. And rules are rules.'

But Perch wasn't paying much attention, as she was scribbling rapidly on a piece of paper.

'I'm sure the warden can sort it out,' said Perch assertively. 'He doesn't want this mess all over the newspapers, does he?' Mr Sentry looked on blankly as Perch leaned over. 'And please make sure Old Velvet gets this note.'

Mr Sentry took the note and ushered Perch quietly through the prison. He opened the main gates and Perch was about to bound through, when she remembered something.

'My lantern,' she said with concern. 'I need my lantern back.' Mr Sentry grabbed it from inside the office, and Perch stepped out into the open air of freedom.

'I kick, I kick you …' echoed around in Perch's head. Slowly the words became clearer.

'I kick you out on your bottom,' she heard. 'You smelly cat, I kick you out on your bottom.' Perch opened her eyes drowsily and was all confused. She looked around at the pots and vases and smelt the sweet burning incense. Her vision came into focus, but only just quickly enough. Bearing down on Perch was an angry-looking Chinese man brandishing a large broom. He took a swipe at Perch but she dodged out of the way and pounced out of the door and onto the pavement. The lantern had taken her back to the Old Curiosity Shop, but Perch was glad to leave it back in the store. The door burst open.

'You come back in my shop,' yelled an irate Fu Kung, 'and I kick your butt!'

Perch legged it round into Christchurch Road, over Crouch Hill and straight down Cecile Park. She tore down the street, startling people along the way, and leapt through the cat-flap back into Charlie's house. She jumped into her basket and pulled the blanket over her head.

After a few moments, Perch realised it felt a bit different in the house. It had been cold when she left but was warm now. And there were voices she didn't recognise. Perch peeped out as two strong hands lifted her up, and Charlie cradled her across his chest.

'I'm *so* happy to see you,' he said lovingly. Perch rubbed her soft fur against Charlie's neck in response.

'Are you OK?' he continued. 'You look terribly sad – like when I first saw you behind bars in the pet shop, all that time ago.' Perch purred comfortingly.

'You've been missing for a week,' said Charlie. 'I've been looking everywhere and have been so worried. So I brought my family down to help.'

Perch glanced over to where Charlie was looking as he started the introductions.

'This is my wife, Anna, and my daughters, Minnie and Leila. And this is my son, Eli. Perch recognised them all immediately from the photos on the mantelpiece. 'Guys,' continued Charlie. 'This is Perch the Cat.'

Perch felt the warmest sense of happiness well up inside her, as small hands gently caressed her. Now she really was part of a family, and she knew in her heart what a lucky cat she was.